"This is a real gamble for you, Sarah, isn't it?" Rafferty asked.

She hesitated, then laughed a bit unsteadily. "Fair warning. I haven't taken many chances in my life. It could blow up in your face."

"I'll take that chance," he told her.

Sarah could feel the slow, pounding pulse of the ocean seeping into her consciousness, as if she was being swept away by something that was beyond her ability to fight. She studied Rafferty's face, fascinated by golden eyes even the moonlight couldn't rob of color or intensity. Her body seemed to have a mind of its own, moving closer to his in response to the touch of his hand on hers.

She stared at his face as it lowered to hers, losing herself in the enigmatic glitter of his eyes. And when warm lips found and captured hers, the heat she felt became molten fire and seared a body that had never known passion's flame.

All her senses went wild as she clung to him. Between one heartbeat and the next was born the overwhelming, mindless need to belong utterly and completely to him. . . .

Bantam Books by Kay Hooper

C.J.'S FATE
(*Loveswept #32*)

SOMETHING DIFFERENT
(*Loveswept #46*)

PEPPER'S WAY
(*Loveswept #62*)

IF THERE BE DRAGONS
(*Loveswept #71*)

ILLEGAL POSSESSION
(*Loveswept #83*)

REBEL WALTZ
(*Loveswept #128*)

TIME AFTER TIME
(*Loveswept #149*)

RAFE, THE MAVERICK
(*Loveswept #163*)

IN SERENA'S WEB
(*Loveswept #189*)

RAVEN ON THE WING
(*Loveswept #193*)

WHAT ARE *LOVESWEPT* ROMANCES?

They are stories of true romance and touching emotion. We believe those two very important ingredients are constants in our highly sensual and very believable stories in the *LOVESWEPT* line. Our goal is to give you, the reader, stories of consistently high quality that may sometimes make you laugh, sometimes make you cry, but are always fresh and creative and contain many delightful surprises within their pages.

Most romance fans read an enormous number of books. Those they truly love, they keep. Others may be traded with friends and soon forgotten. We hope that each *LOVESWEPT* romance will be a treasure—a "keeper." We will always try to publish

LOVE STORIES YOU'LL NEVER FORGET
BY AUTHORS YOU'LL ALWAYS REMEMBER

The Editors

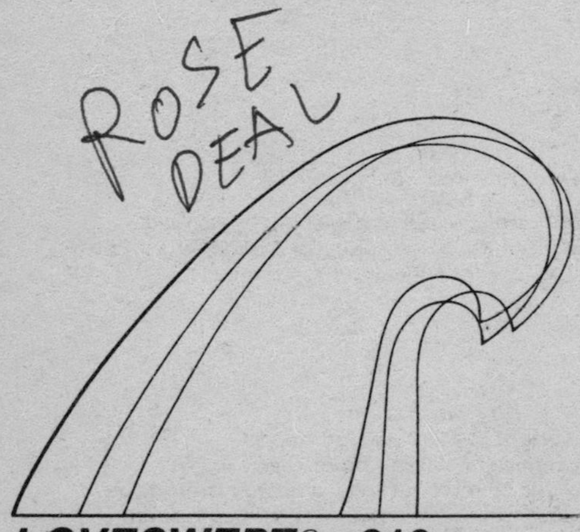

LOVESWEPT® • 219

Kay Hooper

Rafferty's Wife

BANTAM BOOKS
TORONTO • NEW YORK • LONDON • SYDNEY • AUCKLAND

To my brother, Jimmy—
for all those early-morning drives
to the airport

RAFFERTY'S WIFE
A Bantam Book / November 1987

LOVESWEPT® and the wave device are registered trademarks of Bantam Books, Inc. Registered in U.S. Patent and Trademark Office and elsewhere.

ISBN 0-553-21839-5

Published simultaneously in the United States and Canada

Bantam Books are published by Bantam Books, Inc. Its trademark, consisting of the words "Bantam Books" and the portrayal of a rooster, is Registered in U.S. Patent and Trademark Office and in other countries. Marca Registrada. Bantam Books, Inc., 666 Fifth Avenue, New York, New York 10103.

PRINTED IN THE UNITED STATES OF AMERICA

O 0 9 8 7 6 5 4 3 2 1

One

"Why me?"

"Because you're the man I need."

Rafferty Lewis shoved his hands into the pockets of his slacks and stared broodingly out the window. That the view afforded him was the striking expanse of a Trinidad beach cheered him not at all; he would have preferred the New York skyline he normally saw from his office window.

However . . .

"You can refuse, of course, Mr. Lewis. After all, I have no legal claim on you. Not one I'd care to be called on to prove in court, at any rate."

"I'm glad you realize that."

"But you were sworn in as a federal agent, Mr. Lewis. And Mr. Long is willing to give you a leave of absence; since you and your partner

handle all the work for Mr. Long, I took the liberty of inquiring—"

"Hagen, for heaven's sake just tell me what Josh said."

"That you'd be a damned fool to get involved."

"He should know."

Rafferty sighed explosively. A damned fool. Well, he probably was one, since he was here. He didn't like the setup, not one bit, but Hagen had been adamant about it. And, if nothing else, Rafferty had learned respect for Hagen's intelligence, no matter what he thought of his methods. Had Hagen deliberately chosen to approach him when Zach and Lucas—both of whom would probably have tried to dissuade him—were out of touch on business for Josh? For that matter, Josh himself was out of reach on his honeymoon somewhere in the South Pacific. And only Hagen would have had the nerve to intrude at such a time to ask if Josh minded giving up his attorney for a while. Only Hagen would have been able to *find* Josh.

Rafferty smiled. He would have given a lot to have been a fly on the wall during *that* conversation!

It had been just a month or two since the secretive federal agent's machinations had involved them all: Joshua Long, who commanded a formidable financial empire, and the three men who worked for him and were his friends. And at the conclusion of that hectic, troubling, dangerous episode, the wily government agent had managed to draft Josh and his men into "temporary" service.

Temporary my eye! Rafferty thought now. Hagen had intended all along to call in those markers, one by one. He wouldn't get hold of Josh again; Raven, Josh's bride, would see to that, Rafferty guessed. But, he thought ruefully, Hagen had managed to get him.

Thinking of Zach and Lucas, Rafferty decided that Hagen would have a more difficult time enlisting their aid on future assignments. The massive security chief and the shrewd investigator for Joshua Long's empire were tough men. Neither was prone to being backed physically or metaphorically into corners.

As for himself, well, his strongest trait was curiosity. And Hagen had known that. Damn him!

A soft, perhaps timid knock at the door of his suite recalled him to the present, and he turned from the window, unconsciously squaring his shoulders, and headed for the door. With no idea what he would confront, he was braced for the worst. He opened the door, and his golden gift for words, greatly polished by a Harvard education, failed him totally.

"Mr. Lewis? I'm Sarah Cavell."

Rafferty had wondered how on earth he would deal with this particular part of the operation; now he wondered about it again, but for an entirely different reason. Clearing his throat, he hastily stepped back and gestured for Sarah Cavell to enter. "Uh, come in, please."

As she passed him to go into the living room, Rafferty caught a hint of some elusive fragrance that went to his head in an unnerving manner. He felt a sudden strong pulse throb through his body on a wave of heat. Never before had he experienced such an instant, powerful reaction to a woman. It shook him badly.

Still, he was able to put one foot in front of the other to follow her. Barely.

Hagen had offhandedly called Sarah Cavell "attractive."

Hagen, Rafferty decided, badly needed his head examined. Or his eyes.

Sarah was a tiny woman, barely five feet tall if that. And though another woman might have called her petite, no man worth the name would. Her vibrant, surprisingly lush curves of breasts and hips were sure to stop traffic and haunt dreams.

Her hair was that rare, striking color between red and gold, and it hung thick and shining to the middle of her back. Styled simply with a center part, that silky sweep of burnished hair framed a face that was too delicately perfect to be real. She was like a painting; every feature was finely drawn with artistic excellence. And in that strikingly perfect face, her eyes were simply incredible. Huge and shadowed by long, thick lashes, they were a clear, pale green.

In that single, flashing instant, Rafferty wanted Sarah Cavell more than he'd ever wanted anything or anyone in his life. All the training and experience gained in his thirty-four years of living hadn't prepared him for this. His responses were no longer controlled by his mind. Instead, two million years of instincts were in command. His mind grappled with the situation, trying to master instinct, fighting impulses just this side of savage. And the fact that he partially succeeded was due almost entirely to the strength of his own force of will. A complicated situation, he thought grimly, had just become nothing less than impossible. How could he do what he was supposed to?

He waved her to a chair and sat down across from her, hoping his reaction hadn't shown on his face. It was said he had a poker face when he desired one; with any luck at all, that was true. And he was, after all, a lawyer, so he got his tongue in gear. "First names, I think?"

She nodded agreeably. "Unless we want to have people staring at us. That kind of thing perished with formal Victorians." Her soft voice was dry.

"True. So, Sarah, why is a nice girl like you about to spend a few weeks or so with a total stranger?" he asked. Her reaction to his question pierced the fog of his mind. He thought he saw something in her eyes before she answered, something that looked like fear.

"It's my job." She shrugged a little, her green eyes unreadable once more.

Rafferty had learned early in his career that he possessed an innate ability—call it an instinct—to detect anomalies. If something was out of sync in a situation he simply felt it, like an itch at the back of his mind. And that itching was fierce now.

He brushed a thumb along his jaw slowly, watching her, unaware that he was wearing his best professional poker face to hide the turmoil she caused. "Hagen said you'd fill me in," he said abruptly, "on what we're supposed to be doing."

She met his steady gaze, her own unflinching. "Our assignment," she said, "is to make contact with an undercover agent who has coded information. I was pulled—brought in for this—because I'm a cryptographer. Hagen said that twice in the past they've—we've—bought a pig in a poke and found it worthless, so my part in this assignment is to verify the information." Inwardly, Sarah swore at herself, wishing desperately that the handsome face across from her would reveal something of the man behind it, reveal something of his thoughts.

Rafferty noted the lapses and hesitations in her statements, and on top of everything else, he had to wonder. "I see. So we're to sail the Caribbean on this yacht Hagen provided until we make contact with the agent?"

"Yes."

"Why me?" His gaze held her eyes, seeing the flicker of hesitation in their green depths. "Hagen said it was because *I* was the man for the job. As far as I can see, any one of his male agents would have sufficed to provide . . . cover for you."

Sarah's mind recalled an answer to a question she had asked her superior, the same question Rafferty Lewis had just posed.

"Rafferty Lewis was an assistant district attor-

ney at a ridiculously young age," her boss had told her. *"Unfortunately, he had a problem playing political games. Joshua Long hired him, ostensibly to handle his legal affairs. He and his partner do that, of course, but Lewis is also a dollar-a-year man for the government. He's done some work for the Justice Department, and has been in on a couple of crime commissions and task forces. He's a pilot, and he holds a sharpshooter rating with all handguns. He's also extraordinarily cool under pressure and has an ability to fit himself into any situation he encounters. Gets about as nervous as a bag of cement."*

Sarah shook her head slightly, as her thoughts returned to the present. "I can't answer you very well, I'm afraid. Hagen simply told me that you were the best he knew for this assignment."

Rafferty, with recent events very much in mind, shook his head slightly. "That man was born with a motive behind him," he said dryly. "From what I've seen, he has a reason for every action he takes, and every choice he makes. How long have you worked for him?"

"Oh, several years," she said, vague. "But his—our—organization is a large one; I only met him when he briefed me on this assignment."

Rafferty watched her cross slim, tanned legs, reminding himself that he was feeling suspicious and nothing more. Certainly nothing more. But his wayward mind persisted in thinking that she had the most fantastic legs, and what did it matter that she was either lying or concealing something from him?

"Then you"—he cleared his throat of a tendency toward hoarseness. —"have never worked with him personally?"

"No."

Remembering Raven, he asked, "What's your specialty?"

"I told you. I'm a cryptographer."

"Puzzles, coded messages and information—like that?"

"Like that."

All Rafferty's instincts, legal and otherwise, warned him that he'd better get all the information he could before this thing began. Past experience told him there might well be little time for it later. At the moment, however, he couldn't think of many questions to ask. Except the ones he couldn't ask, the ones he wanted very badly to ask, the ones having nothing to do with the assignment.

"Did you love your husband very much?"

"Can you forget him?"

"Could you want me?"

He cleared his throat again. "I see. Well, if I have the sequence of events correctly, we're to check into another hotel here in Trinidad for a couple of days, then board the yacht and set sail for some country. . . . What was it?"

"Kadeira. It's northwest of here."

"Yes, I've heard of it. And while we sail around Kadeira, we're supposed to make contact with the operative with the coded information?"

She hesitated. "Um . . . sort of. Actually, the agent is more or less incommunicado because of his cover. We have to go to him."

Rafferty drummed his long fingers soundlessly on the arm of his chair as he forced himself to consider this second disconcerting aspect of the situation. And he knew now why Hagen had been so evasive in naming their destination. Rafferty would have laughed in his face if he'd been told they were actually to go into Kadeira. "Correct me if I'm wrong," he said morosely, "but isn't Kadeira having political and social difficulties at the moment? The kinds of difficulties which make it inadvisable for tourists to visit the island?"

She was chewing her bottom lip, drawing his gaze despite all his good intentions and nagging suspicions, causing his heart to pound heavily and every muscle of his body to tighten, and her soft voice sounded as if it were afraid of itself.

"Uh, yes. The president there claims it isn't a revolution and that he's in control, but there have been a few incidents in the past months involving American tourists. They don't get many tourists," she added.

His fingers drummed faster. Dammit, why couldn't he take his eyes off her? "Yes. As I recall from the news reports, a salesman from Wichita was arrested for being a spy. Bit paranoid, aren't they?"

She looked uneasy for a moment. "He was released," she offered.

"Uh-huh. But the toy manufacturer from Billings hasn't been seen in over a month."

Her eyes widened, but Sarah Cavell had nothing to say.

Rafferty stopped drumming long enough to run his fingers through his thick copper hair. His tawny eyes frowned at her. "Tell me, did Hagen suggest we go into this island paradise armed? Or are we being given diplomatic immunity to perform an act that Kadeira's president—judging by his record—would certainly consider an act of espionage?"

Sarah examined her long, bronze-lacquered nails. "About guns, personal choice, Hagen said. I should mention, I couldn't hit the side of a barn if I was standing next to it."

"Great," Rafferty muttered, becoming unwillingly fascinated in a horrified kind of way. "And the rest?"

She seemed to find the secrets of the universe in the metallic gleam of her nails. "Oh . . . no diplomatic or political immunity for us, I'm afraid. Kadeira doesn't exactly recognize American nationals as being . . . worthy of such honors. We're reasonably safe outside the three-mile limit, but once inside Kadeira . . ."

"And how," Rafferty asked carefully, "are we supposed to get inside Kadeira? Being unworthy American nationals, I mean?"

"Hagen said that it's been arranged."

"Oh, did he? Did he happen to mention just *how* it's been arranged?"

"No."

Rafferty began to entertain notions of locating the elusive Hagen and choking the information out of him. It was a blissful possibility while it lasted. He sighed. "I see. We just leap blindly into this thing, trusting Hagen beyond the limits of sanity. Do you happen to speak Spanish?" He watched her shake her head slowly, and wasn't surprised. "Neither do I. And from what I've seen of the rare news footage, neither of us looks as if we belong in Kadeira. How in the name of hell are we supposed to get into that country without getting ourselves arrested?"

Sarah lifted her hands in a kind of shrug and tried a smile that she couldn't quite pull off. "Hagen said it's all arranged," she repeated softly.

Rafferty wished he smoked. Or drank to excess. Any escape would have been pleasant at the moment. "Right. Well, ignoring that question for the moment, what about later? Once we're inside Kadeira, how do we make contact with the agent holding the information?"

Sarah studied her nails again. "We'll receive a signal from him to arrange a meeting. At the meeting, we'll receive the information, which I'm to verify. Then we just . . . leave Kadeira."

"Just leave Kadeira," Rafferty repeated, fascinated. "Tell me—since I definitely have a need to know—just what is this information we're going after?"

She sent him a fleeting glance. In a very soft voice, she replied, "It has to do with an organization operating out of Kadeira."

"What *kind* of organization?" he asked with careful politeness.

Sarah was chewing her lip again. "Terrorist."

Rafferty closed his eyes briefly. If she chewed her lip once more, he decided, he was going to lunge. He could certainly think of worse ways to begin what was looking more and more like a nightmare. "That's what I was afraid of. So. We're going after information which, if we are caught, will clearly brand us both as spies and will certainly get us shot—at the very least. And our fearless leader Hagen will no doubt call out the marines if we're arrested and labeled as spies?"

She brought her nails closer to her face and gazed at them, frowning. "Well . . . there are problems with that. We aren't supposed to be conducting covert operations down there. And we would—legally—be in the wrong if we were caught." She linked her fingers together, resting them in her lap, and lifted pleading green eyes to his face. "So we're pretty much on our own, I'm afraid."

Rafferty tried to resist those eyes. He *really* tried. But somehow he found all his wrathful dismay seeping slowly from his trained legal mind. His trained legal mind, in fact, seemed disposed to make fanciful and utterly ridiculous comparisons between green eyes and absurd things like priceless gems and bottomless lagoons.

"I think—" He cleared his throat violently and tried again. "I think we're both fools."

Sarah Cavell, watching that lean and handsome face, silently had to agree. With her part of it, at least. She was a fool. She was a fool because a stranger had opened a hotel room door, and looked down at her with surprised tawny gold eyes, and she had forgotten why she was there. She had forgotten the assignment, the dangers, and her own serious lack of training for situations such as this promised to be.

She had all but forgotten her name.

What she had not forgotten, what Hagen had impressed on her strongly, was that Rafferty Lewis was off-limits. He would be her professional partner for the next three weeks or so, but any other involvement was impossible. He had, Hagen had told her quietly, buried a young wife only a few months before. A much-beloved wife. But she wasn't to mention that, because Rafferty had not recovered from his loss, would probably never recover.

Sarah was only dimly aware of hot tears welling up in her eyes at the thought. Hers was a soft heart, unsuited to the work ahead of her, and she tended to cry for anyone burdened with pain. She wanted to cry for Rafferty's young wife, and for him, but blinked back the tears fiercely; not for anything would she expose the man's raw grief to even her own compassion. Meeting his eyes, she found them rather startled, and realized he had seen the unshed tears. She spoke quickly. "I guess we should find the other hotel, then."

"I guess so. My bags are waiting downstairs."

She rose to her feet, absently smoothing the pale cream silk dress that complemented her golden tan so well. "I'll—I'll get a cab for us and wait outside."

Still disturbed by her tears, Rafferty wracked

his brain to remember what had been said to upset her. Heaven knew he didn't want her to cry. Tears in those vivid green eyes roused strange feelings inside him. It was worse than watching small white teeth bite into a full lower lip.

He couldn't think what could have made her cry. Unless . . . Was she worried that he might refuse to accompany her? Or had he inadvertently said something to remind her of her recent tragic loss? Frustrated, he could think of no way to ask without bringing it out into the open, and he had promised Hagen. . . .

At a luxurious hotel on the other end of Trinidad, Mr. and Mrs. Rafferty Lewis checked in late that Friday afternoon. They were accompanied by mounds of baggage, and it was obvious that they were, if not a honeymoon couple, then at the very least newly wed and still delighted with marriage. The bride wore a spectacular diamond beside her gold wedding band, and the groom wore his own wide band with pride.

However, the status of the couple might have undergone a change in the eyes of the hotel staff if any had overheard the groom's hissed words in the elevator going up to their suite on the twentieth floor.

"Why do we have to start this *now*?"

Sarah gazed at the bellman's back and said nothing, but Rafferty's question brought the quick, inevitable tears to her eyes. Hagen, she thought, should be shot for subjecting this poor man to such a charade. It was cruel. Anyone with even a shade of sensitivity must have *known* how hard it would be on Rafferty to pretend a loving, happy marriage so soon after his own was destroyed.

She said nothing, fighting to suppress her compassion while the bellman brought their bags into the large suite, and she wandered about the rooms automatically exclaiming at the view and the lovely decor. She listened as Rafferty thanked and dismissed the man.

Then she turned and faced her "husband"—for the duration.

Keeping her voice even with an effort, she said, "According to all the information Hagen—we—have, there shouldn't be any undue suspicion directed toward us. But there's no reason to take a chance on that. There's too much at stake. We have to make sure our cover is solid. So we begin now. And we keep it up until this is over. Hagen believes it's vitally important that no one question our marriage."

Rafferty moved toward the window and stared out, looking at anything else because looking at her affected him oddly. "And if someone does question it? I suppose our marriage has been duly documented and registered?"

"Yes, it has. We were married two months ago in New York, after a whirlwind courtship."

"How romantic." He didn't intend to sound so sarcastic, but Rafferty was still incensed with Hagen for choosing such a cover for Sarah. The callous bastard!

Sarah dropped her purse on a loveseat nearby

and sent a glance through the doorway into the bedroom; it boasted a king-size bed, but she felt it wasn't big enough. Not big enough, at any rate, for a man and woman separated by a charade and a tragedy one of them had suffered.

"There's still time for you to turn the assignment down," she reminded him quietly. "Hagen very likely has someone else waiting in the wings in case you do. He has a reputation for not leaving much to chance."

He turned slowly toward her, his face still. His gaze moved from her burnished hair to her small feet, taking in every delicate feature and the throat-tightening curves in between. "No, I suppose he doesn't." Rafferty drew a breath. "Well, he believes I'm the man for the job, for whatever reasons. So I'm in. We'll spend the next two days here, and then board the yacht. What's it called, by the way?"

Sarah linked her fingers together. "An odd name for a yacht. It's called the *Thespian.*"

Rafferty's eyes narrowed, but a smile curved his lips. "Maybe not so strange. We're actors—I suppose the yacht is as well."

Sarah's gaze skittered away from that smile, and she reminded herself again of why they were here and what their relationship was to one another. Professional partners. Actors playing roles. For the duration.

He cleared his throat, not surprised that it was beginning to feel raw from all the tightening and clearing he was doing. Nodding toward the bar in one corner, he suggested, "Drinks?"

Sarah sat on the loveseat, wondering a bit desperately how she could possibly get through this without making a fool of herself. It didn't look especially promising. "Please. Anything will do." She watched beneath her lashes while he poured their drinks, her gaze clinging to broad shoulders, and long-fingered hands that moved with natural grace. When he brought her glass, she took pains to avoid touching him, so much so that of course she *did* touch his fingers and nearly dropped her drink.

Rafferty didn't seem to notice. He sat at the other end of the loveseat, her purse the only barrier between them, and half turned to face her. "I don't suppose it's necessary that we know much about each other," he said slowly, "but we'd probably be more comfortable if we do. Do you agree?"

She nodded. Rattled, she spoke at random. "Yes, I—Probably. Hagen said you were once a district attorney."

He nodded. "Once. But I wasn't exactly suited to playing political games. So when a businessman asked me to work for him, I jumped at the chance."

"Joshua Long."

"Yes. Since you know the name, you probably know he's a financial wizard. My partner and I handle most of his legal problems, not that there are many considering the size of his empire. He has other interests, though, and so does his half sister, whose legal work we also handle."

"Other interests? I heard that he was not only

philanthropic, but also involved in fighting things most people aren't even aware exist."

Rafferty laughed a little. "I suppose that's one way of putting it. Josh hates dishonesty and believes everyone should fight against anything that's wrong. *He* does. And, because I work for him, I've had occasion to fight as well."

Sarah sipped her drink and smiled, feeling more relaxed now. "According to your file," she went on, "you've fought a few times on your own. And for the Justice Department. On crime commissions. You went undercover as a special agent once to gather information on corruption in a state-level attorney general's office, didn't you?"

He nodded, but said dismissively, "I had the background for the job. Still, it was satisfying to be able to do something about a serious problem. I guess that's why you're in this business?"

Sarah wasn't evasive, but her tone was offhand. "I've always been good with puzzles, and that's an ability that people tend to notice even before you leave school. Hagen's people found me in college, and when I graduated there was a job waiting for me." She looked at him for a moment, then added dryly, "An *office* job, I'm afraid."

Rafferty swallowed part of his drink. He needed it. Then he looked at her. "In other words, you've never had a field assignment before this?"

"That sums it up nicely."

"I was hoping," he murmured, "that at least one of us knew what we were doing."

"Sorry."

He sighed and tried not to feel appalled. "So you sit in an office and unravel puzzles?"

"More or less. Decipher messages, break codes, invent them and transcribe them. Things like that. And I'm Information Retrieval too."

Rafferty blinked. "Is that what I think it is?"

"Probably. In our office—which is disguised as a research company, by the way—you come to me for answers. About anything. Want to know how much grain the U.S. has stockpiled? Just ask me. Want to know how many passenger miles are flown by the world's aircraft each year? I can answer that for you. Want to know the total cost of obscure research projects on such topics as why cats purr? I'm the one you ask."

Fascinated, Rafferty said, "Computer data banks?"

"If I need them. I don't, often." Her smile was faint. "I have an unusual memory."

"Unusual in what way?" He thought he knew.

"I remember things. In fact, I remember everything I've ever read or heard or seen. And I see patterns in things; that's why I'm a good cryptographer."

He stared at her for a moment, then asked briskly, "What's the population of New York City?"

Without hesitation and in an automatic tone, she replied, "Seven million, seventy-one thousand, six hundred thirty-nine, according to the 1980 census."

Refusing to admit defeat, Rafferty wracked his brain for trivia. It distracted him from other things. "The Cougar Dam is on what river?"

"The South Fork McKenzie River. It's in Oregon. Constructed in 1964." Sarah was beginning to smile.

"Who's on the one-hundred-thousand-dollar bill?"

She blinked. "Wilson. Have you been associating with the Treasury Department or Federal Reserve System? They're the only ones who see that one."

He ignored the question. "Who invented the third-rail system used in subways?"

"Granville T. Woods."

"Who was the twenty-fifth *Vice President* of the U.S.?"

"Theodore Roosevelt."

Rafferty closed his eyes. "And I suppose you can tell me who made a trip around the world in 1889?"

"Nellie Bly. Seventy-two days, six hours, eleven minutes."

Rafferty finished his drink. It seemed appropriate. "I can see," he stated, "why you're such an asset to Hagen. I bet you read very fast too."

She shrugged. "Well, I don't always read; I just look. Statistics mostly, going as far back as there were records. You have to understand, I've been doing this as long as I can remember. Teachers used to accuse me of cheating, until I proved to them that I remembered facts verbatim."

After a moment, Rafferty said slowly, "I imagine that was difficult for you. Being different from other kids."

Sarah smiled faintly. "Yes. But my parents were

terrific. They made me feel that I had a gift rather than a curse. It helped make . . . other opinions . . . easier to take."

Rafferty nodded. "And so you grew up to become the answer person for a secret government agency."

"There are worse jobs."

"Agreed." Rafferty stirred, abruptly restless. "I don't know about you, but I'm starved. Since we're supposed to be visible, why don't we go out somewhere for dinner?"

"That sounds good." She rose to her feet and then hesitated, glancing toward the bedroom.

Rafferty got up and said matter-of-factly, "I'll call for reservations while you get ready, all right?"

"Fine." Avoiding his eyes, she went into the bedroom and closed the door. Leaning back against it, Sarah swore very softly.

At least her make-believe husband had some experience in sharing bed and bath with a partner; she felt distinctly uncomfortable and embarrassed about the entire situation. What was the protocol, for heaven's sake? Did they draw straws or flip a coin to decide who used the shower first? And what about the bed?

What, indeed! She doubted that Hagen would approve of a call to housekeeping for an extra pillow and blanket so that one member of the happily married couple could bunk down on the couch.

Uncertain as to how long it was supposed to take for her to change, Sarah hastily unpacked toilet articles and a dress suitable for evening dining, then went into the bathroom and stepped into the shower.

On top of the practical worries inherent in the situation were other concerns. Under orders from Hagen, she had kept certain information to herself, and she wasn't happy about doing that. It was alien to her nature to deceive anyone, and secrecy placed an added strain on nerves that were already stretched taut.

Sarah was still a bit bewildered at being in the middle of this; she couldn't recall exactly how it had all come about. Somehow or other, Hagen had made it seem utterly natural that she should be the "operative" involved.

Her unusual life had made her somewhat introverted, shy, and unsure of herself in many ways. She spent too much time alone. There hadn't been a lack of masculine offers in her past, but her natural reserve had nipped many overtures in the bud, and her lack of self-confidence had prevented her from opening up with others.

This situation was totally foreign to her from beginning to end. She had no idea how to play the part assigned to her, and was half frightened at the thought of living in such intimacy with a stranger, even if that stranger *did* attract her. Especially *because* that stranger attracted her.

There was something about Rafferty Lewis, something . . . leashed. His features were handsome, set off by those extraordinary gold eyes. Like herself, he apparently tanned instead of freckled, despite being a redhead. He was tall and broad-shouldered, and moved gracefully. He was quite obviously intelligent, and his voice was deep and warm.

But none of that quite explained what Sarah felt, what she sensed, when she looked at him. For all his cool intelligence and relaxed physical movements, what Sarah sensed was power. Not the power of sheer muscle, but something else, something far more understated, and therefore much more dangerous. It was the power of an iron will and a dynamic personality.

Some men, she thought shrewdly, would underrate him because of that, failing to glimpse what lay beneath his almost lazy surface. But she doubted that many women would make that mistake. More intuitive than men, most women would sense something powerful within Rafferty. She made a mental notc to ask him if he had tangled with women attorneys in his work and, if so, who had won. She was curious to discover if her assessment of him was close to the mark. She thought it was. And, believing that, she had to wonder about the next few weeks even more. How would Rafferty react to the deceptions and the dangers?

Troubled and nervous, Sarah quickly dried off after her shower and dressed in the coral silk dress she had chosen. She piled her long hair loosely atop her head and secured it with a few pins, then hastily applied makeup with an unsteady hand. Perfume was an afterthought, as were the diamond studs in her ears. Then she studied herself in the long mirror on the bedroom closet door. What she saw gave her no courage at all.

She looked scared to death, she decided. She drew several deep breaths, trying to vanquish the fright in her green eyes, trying to square her shoulders and straighten her spine.

Then she turned and headed for the other room.

What was she *doing* here?

Two

What was he *doing* here?

Rafferty fixed himself another drink and went over to the window, no more pleased than before to confront the sparkling white expanse of beach outside. He wasn't happy. What was he doing here pretending to be married to a woman he'd just met, and about to stroll casually into a hostile country to retrieve stolen information?

Damn Hagen!

He could admit the truth to himself. And the truth was that he was less bothered by the coming foray into Kadeira than he was by his pretended marriage to Sarah. Only a fool, of course, would have discounted the dangers of going into Kadeira, and Rafferty wasn't a fool. He had found himself in physical danger before and knew that his instincts and reactions were good, reliable. And that was all a man could depend on.

But the minefields laid all around this make-believe marriage promised a more thorough danger to his peace of mind.

How on earth could he pretend an intimacy he wanted to be real? How could he force himself to consider this a necessary arrangement with no personal feelings involved, when it wasn't?

He could, he thought, make a decent stab at being a husband, and his own feelings would look convincing because they were based on a strong reality. But what would his performance and her own do to Sarah? And what about all the practical little problems?

Half turning, Rafferty measured the couch with his eyes and sighed. Great. He'd end up permanently crippled if he slept there. And what about aboard the *Thespian*? Luxurious though it could prove to be, he doubted the yacht would boast a couch of any size, and the possibility of two beds in one cabin was doubtful. And they were supposed to be *married*, dammit. Happily married. Which meant they should share a bed.

He turned back to the window and lifted a hand to drum his fingers absently against the pane. How did Sarah really feel about the situation? She seemed to consider it merely a part of her job, yet he had seen uncertainty—and perhaps fear—in her vivid eyes. And tears. Rafferty felt a stirring inside him then as he remembered her tears, and he absorbed the sensation with something near wonder.

An impossible situation? Dear heaven . . .

He had, in some vague part of his mind, always

assumed that he would one day fall in love. That some positive fate would grab him by the shoulder and point, saying, "That's the one." Yet he had watched a close friend lose the control built over a lifetime and flounder in a desperate emotional turmoil when fate had grabbed him, and Rafferty had assured himself that his own way would be easier.

So much for certainty.

Fate had grabbed him and pointed, gleefully, to a woman who had recently and tragically lost a cherished husband. To a woman whose job it was to pretend Rafferty was her beloved husband for a few weeks, so that they could slip into a dangerous place to retrieve dangerous secrets.

Blindly, Rafferty stared out the window. Weeks.

He felt an impulse to turn and walk away from both the situation and the woman, but knew that the action would solve little, even if it were possible. And it wasn't possible. Not now. He was trapped, not by patriotism, not because he had given his word, not even because he hated terrorism with a vengeance. He was trapped because there was nothing in him that would allow him to walk away from *her.*

A rational man, whose profession had instilled in him strong emotional control and taught him the benefits of cultivating an easy and unthreatening body language, Rafferty wasn't prone to letting his emotions dictate his actions. But now, even though reason told him to walk away, emotions refused to grant him that logical solution.

"Did you make reservations?"

Rafferty turned slowly to look at her, wondering if his face looked as stiff as it felt. He thought it probably did. He gazed at the slender, curved body caressed by coral silk, at shimmering hair arranged in a curiously seductive, yet innocent style. He looked at the delicate face, lovely and poignant, into pale green eyes shadowed with nervousness.

He remembered reading somewhere that men made their own hells, and now he agreed with that. Hagen might have shaped this one and cannily tempted him to enter, but Rafferty had made it his own. Finishing his drink, he set the glass aside and headed for the bedroom door. "Reservations for seven. I'll get ready." He wondered if his voice sounded as hoarse to her as it did to him.

Sarah stood very still in the center of the room, looking at nothing, hearing the door close quietly behind him. They couldn't go on like this, she thought wildly. She was no actress, and it was clear that Rafferty was disturbed by the pretense surrounding them. They were strangers, and she was very conscious of her reaction to him, very aware of its futility.

Pretense . . . they were surrounded by it. Pretending they were newlyweds, pretending this trip was an innocent one. How were they supposed to do their job with so many tensions straining between them?

During dinner in an elegant restaurant, it became obvious to her that Rafferty had come to the same conclusions. He began talking quietly, looking at everything but her, clearly trying to ease the tension between them.

"Hagen threw us into this," he said, "and he obviously felt we could be successful; if nothing else, I've learned to respect the man's judgment. So it's up to us to work out some way of playing our parts effectively. Agreed?"

She toyed with her wine glass. "Agreed."

When Rafferty continued it was in a cautious tone. "I'm sure we both realize that it's . . . needless under the circumstances to venture too far into each other's pasts. What we have to concern ourselves with is the present. That's all that matters."

Sarah nodded.

"We're in an awkward situation, forced to pretend, and all we really know about each other is what we've been told by Hagen." Rafferty frowned suddenly.

Seeing only the frown, Sarah spoke hurriedly. "I'm sure we can work out something agreeable to both of us."

Rafferty stared at her then, and she saw a puzzled, hesitant look in his eyes. "Yes." He spoke slowly. "Yes, I'm sure we can, Sarah. My name, by the way, is Rafferty."

A little startled, Sarah realized that she had yet to call him by name. "I—I know. It's an unusual name."

He was silent, waiting.

After a moment, she repeated, "Rafferty."

He nodded, but still seemed to hesitate, watching her. Then he spoke in the same slow tone as before. "We have to maintain the illusion of a happily married couple, which will place certain demands on us. We'll be expected to be relaxed and at ease with each other at the very least. Be expected to—touch each other. Expected to share a bed."

Rafferty noted that her eyes skittered away from his and that a faint flush lightly colored her cheeks. But what he had expected to see in her eyes was absent. He began to wonder, with a surge of hope that made him dizzy and threatened to block his throat.

"Yes. I understand that."

"It'll be harder on the boat," he said softly. "Closer quarters, more intimate surroundings."

"Yes, I—I know."

"Are you afraid of me, Sarah?"

She started. Her eyes lifted to his and widened. "It isn't that. I just—I've never *done* anything like this before! I don't know how to pretend, what to say or do . . ."

"No—experience of being married?"

Puzzled by something in his voice, Sarah shook her head. "No, of course not." To her astonishment, Rafferty suddenly grinned, and it was an expression of heartfelt relief.

"That's what I thought. Damn Hagen. I'll strangle him if I ever get my hands on him! Now I know how Josh felt."

Sarah stared at him, then felt a peculiar uncertainty. "You mean he told you I was married?"

"Widowed," Rafferty confirmed dryly. "And recently."

She began to feel less uncertain, definitely used, and ridiculously happy. If Hagen had told Rafferty that *she* was widowed . . . "Have—have you ever been—?"

"Married? No. Let me guess. He told you I had been? A tragic story, and you weren't supposed to mention it to me?"

"Yes. Exactly." Sarah let out pent-up breath in a long sigh. "Take a number. I'm going to strangle him *first.*"

Laughing, Rafferty shook his head. "I should have guessed sooner. I have it on the best authority that Hagen is as devious as a barrel of snakes."

"But why would he do such a thing? I don't understand his motives."

"I think I do." Rafferty explained how he had come to meet the government agent, and how Hagen had nearly gotten himself throttled by a furious Josh Long because he had neglected to share certain information. "Maybe it was just his mania for secrecy, but whatever the reason he kept us all in the dark about too many facts, and in so doing, put the woman Josh loved in danger—unsuspecting danger. When Hagen finally told us all the truth, Josh went berserk. It was understandable, but Hagen hadn't thought of that.

"It was the personal factor that threw him," he finished. "He'd forgotten—or maybe just didn't think—that people deeply involved with one another don't always react predictably. I'll bet he decided to prevent that possibility this time by making each of us believe there was no chance of personal involvement. He intended us to be totally professional about this assignment, and told both of us things he believed would achieve that end."

It made sense in a roundabout way, Sarah decided. Finding Rafferty's gaze fixed intently on her, she concentrated on her wine glass. "I suppose," she said, "he meant it for the best. I mean . . . we have to get that information. And there isn't much time. I've heard that—that getting involved with someone undercover is like a shipboard romance. It only lasts until you return to your home port."

"Unless you want it to last longer."

She stirred in her chair, restless and uneasy. "I suppose. But undercover operations, like trips on board ships, tend to intensify time spent together. It isn't *natural* time. The circumstances tend to make people feel things they wouldn't otherwise have felt. That's dangerous. And—and painful when the trip comes to an end."

"Josh and Raven are on their honeymoon," he told her.

"There's always an exception to the rule. But rarely more than one."

"Warning me?" he asked gently.

Sarah didn't want to meet his gaze, but something compelled her to. She wondered, vaguely, how it was possible for a man to have such golden eyes. "Maybe I'm warning myself," she confessed almost inaudibly. "I'm out of my element on this assignment, Rafferty. It'll be hard enough to cope with that."

He drew a deep breath. "I understand. At least something in me understands. But I don't think I can be professionally detached about this, Sarah." He hesitated, then said, "I want you."

Swallowing hard, she felt heat uncurl within her, spreading outward from some previously undiscovered core deep inside and sending warm ripples all the way through her. She could suddenly feel her heart beating in her throat, each throb an echo of his blunt statement.

"Sarah?"

She glanced around at the dim restaurant, bewildered by her own feelings, by the temptation to follow impulse for the first time in her life. "What—what am I supposed to say to that?" she asked, and the confusion in her voice was real.

His soft laugh was a little unsteady. "Say that I'm not the only one feeling more than a professional interest in my partner."

She met his gaze, her own disturbed. She wondered if she was prepared for this, and knew she wasn't. There was no distinction in her mind between heart and body; they were two halves of one in her experience. What her body felt was an echo of her heart's yearning and . . . dear heaven, that was hazardous.

And shocking in its unexpectedness.

Her voice, soft and stark, emerged without her conscious control. "I had a friend who was a field agent. And she was good. Very, very good. She had years of experience, lightning reflexes, and wonderful instincts. For a special assignment, she was paired with someone from outside the agency."

She hesitated, then went on. "Our agency . . . well, what we do isn't written down anywhere.

Reports are verbal, not taped or put on paper. Certain necessary messages are sent to base in code, then decoded. As soon as they reach the proper level, they're destroyed. If—if I hadn't been decoding that day, I would never have known exactly what had happened."

Rafferty thought he knew. "What happened?"

Sarah's eyes filled with tears as she remembered. "It wasn't her partner's fault. It wasn't *her* fault. Except that . . . she had gotten emotionally involved with him. Walked into a trap because her mind wasn't on her work. She was able to send a last message, taking the blame. She was the pro; she should have *known*. But she hadn't been careful. And neither of them came home."

Reaching across the table, Rafferty covered her restless hand with his own. Gently, he said, "Answer something honestly for me, Sarah." He waited for her hesitant nod, then said, "I'm not the only one feeling more than a professional interest in my partner, am I?"

Sarah looked down at their hands, seeing her fingers twine with his without her conscious volition. She wanted desperately to lie to him, but she just couldn't somehow. Almost whispering, she said, "No."

His fingers tightened, but his voice remained quiet and gentle. "Then that's something we have to deal with. The human element, Sarah. We didn't ask for it. Given a choice, I doubt that either of us would pick now, this situation, to become involved with each other. But it's happening."

"Rafferty—"

"It's happening, Sarah. And in our particular situation, we can't ignore it. Given our cover, fighting this would be the worst possible thing we could do. We're supposed to be a happily married couple."

She saw his point, but remained unconvinced. He didn't know, didn't know it all. What they had to do. "And if things get bad? Either between us or—or with the assignment? Don't you see that one or both of us could get killed if at all times we aren't keeping our minds on what we're supposed to be doing?"

There was a moment of silence, and then Rafferty quickly sat back and signaled for the check. Sarah, her eyes down and her hands feeling strangely cold, said nothing and made no objection when they rose from the table and left the restaurant. He had chosen a place near their hotel, within walking distance, but once they were outside he guided her toward the beach, at this hour a pale strip in the moonlight.

Sarah paused once to remove her sandals, accepting his supporting hand in the same silence with which it was offered, then walked wordlessly beside him. The beach was nearly deserted. There were only a few couples strolling along, presumably taking advantage of the moonlight and the muffled roar of the ocean that provided an atmosphere of romantic intimacy.

It made Sarah's heart ache.

Finally Rafferty spoke, his tone conversational but strained. "As I see it, we have two choices. Either one or both of us pull out, or else we go on.

I'm not pulling out without you, Sarah. And I have a feeling you mean to go on with this assignment."

"Yes."

"Then we go on. Together." He found her free hand with his own, and their fingers laced together instantly. "And we deal with this."

Walking beside him across sand damp from the last high tide, sand unmarked because no one else had chosen to walk just where they walked, Sarah felt a curious and unfamiliar sense of fatalism. Despite everything, the pretenses and dangers, despite Hagen's determined attempts to prevent an involvement between them, something had drawn them together almost instantly.

Gazing down at the damp, blank sand, she thought of a Robert Frost poem. Both of them, she thought, were looking at a forked road that was all but unmarked. A road neither had walked before.

No matter which they chose, regrets were likely, even inevitable. But Sarah thought that she would regret it more if they chose the safer, well-trodden path. She had always taken the safe way, the sure and predictable way, the familiar way. Until this assignment.

For once in her life she had followed an impulse undoubtedly created by Hagen, choosing to leave her safe office for the dangerous waters of a dangerous game. She had chosen. And she had met Rafferty. Hours ago. Only hours? If so much in her life could change within hours, how much more during weeks? And she wanted change. She realized then that she wanted change with everything inside her.

Anyone who knew her would have laughed uncontrollably at the mere thought of Sarah Cavell being incautious. Cautious, they would have said, didn't begin to describe her. And there had been nothing in her experience to jolt her from the safe and predictable niche she had made of her life.

"Yes," she said suddenly.

Rafferty looked down at her by his side, seeing something in her moonlit face he hadn't expected, yet somehow wasn't surprised by. The delicate beauty was still there, the poignancy remained. But her expression was subtly different. The smile curving her lips was reckless.

He drew them to a stop, turning so that they faced each other. "I know we're taking a chance with all this," he said huskily. "We don't know anything about each other. But I think we'll learn all we need to know during the next few weeks. Maybe by the time our ship reaches its home port. . ."

She looked up at him, still smiling. "It'll be the beginning instead of the end? Maybe. The only thing I'm sure of, Rafferty, is that when I walk off that ship, I have to know that I took full advantage of the voyage."

His free hand lifted to touch her cheek, skimming over soft flesh until it lay against her neck. Whimsically, he said, "I get the feeling this is more of a gamble for you than it seems on the surface."

She hesitated, then laughed a bit unsteadily. "It

is. Fair warning—I don't think I know myself very well. I haven't taken many chances in my life. It could blow up in your face."

"I'll take that chance," he told her.

Sarah could feel the slow, pounding pulse of the ocean seeping into her consciousness as though some invisible dam was being eroded. It was like nothing she'd ever felt before, as if she were being swept away by something that was beyond her ability to fight. She stared up at his face, unconsciously marking each feature in her mind, fascinated by golden eyes even the moonlight couldn't rob of color or intensity. Her body seemed to have a mind of its own, stepping nearer to his in response to the gentle pressure of his hand.

She barely heard her own breath catch when her body touched his. She was too involved with the abrupt rush of sensation stinging every nerve ending. After the first gasp she couldn't seem to breathe, and despite the barriers of her silk dress and the fine linen of his white shirt, she could feel the heat of his flesh when her breasts touched his chest.

He had released her hand, his own moving to the small of her back to press her even nearer, and her hands lifted to slide beneath his jacket and encircle his lean waist, her shoes falling unheeded to the sand.

Sarah found her eyes focusing on his lips, and she felt a strange transformation beginning inside her. The tentative heat that had uncurled earlier at his blunt statement of desire seemed to spread now and intensify, flowing throughout her limbs, filling her until she was conscious of nothing but warmth and a slow pounding pulse that echoed the ocean's eternal rhythm.

"Sarah . . ."

She stared at his face as it lowered to hers, losing herself in the enigmatic glitter of his eyes. And when warm lips found and captured her own, liquid heat became molten fire and seared a body that had never before known passion's flame. She was lost, totally and completely lost, and her astonishment was a small, frail thing in the face of her overwhelming response.

She could taste the ocean's salt mist and feel its cool dampness in the ever-present breeze off the water. The pounding of the surf seemed louder in her ears, elemental in her veins. The moonlight stole color from everything but his eyes, his glittering, compelling eyes.

Her chest hurt, and she wasn't certain if it was because she couldn't seem to breathe or because her breasts were crushed against his hard chest. But there was pleasure even in the ache, and Sarah was shocked that a man's body pressed to her own could feel so wonderful. She could feel muscles in his back rippling beneath her fingers, and when his legs widened she instinctively moved closer, between them, her body molding itself to his.

All her senses went wild as she clung to him, rational thought seared away. Between one heartbeat and the next was born the overwhelming, mindless need to belong utterly and completely to him. Nothing else mattered. Her body craved his with the madness of starvation. Every inch of her flesh throbbed to life, and if she had been capable of thought she would have realized then that the possibility of dealing with this had never existed.

There had been nothing tentative in that first kiss, nothing hesitant. It was the touch of a lover, bold and demanding. Her response, instant and total, wrenched a smothered groan from Rafferty, and his lips slanted across hers to deepen that bold touch with growing hunger.

Her mouth was warm and responsive, and he could feel the way her body moved unconsciously and instinctively to be closer to his. His heart thudded in a quickening rhythm, the rhythm spreading outward to heat his flesh and clench his muscles in a spasm of need. The thin silk dress she wore was a tactile delight, the material sliding across her skin as his hand moved over her back and down to mold her hips, and his swelling body ached with the warm yielding contact of hers.

Rafferty had forgotten where they were; it didn't seem to matter. The rush and pounding of the ocean was no more than a subliminal reminder of the surging desire he felt, drowning out other sounds even as his passion drowned out all reason. The taste of her lips was sweet as wine, the scent of her something heady, warmly potent, and her soft, curved body seduced him wildly.

And when the first crash of thunder came, Rafferty hardly recognized it as something outside the stormy world their embrace had created. But a sudden gust of wind, tasting strongly of salt and decidedly wet, all but knocked them from their feet, and startled gazes met in near darkness when the moonlight was blotted out by fast-moving clouds.

They were drenched before they could even step apart, the capricious wind whipping madly at their clothing and snatching Sarah's hair loose from the pins that had held it. Lightning split the sky, and Rafferty bent quickly to get her shoes. While cold rain beat at them, they raced back up the beach holding hands, fighting wind and wet to get to their hotel.

They were laughing when they ducked inside the door of the lobby, even as others caught by the storm were laughing. Sarah wasn't the only guest to reach shelter barefoot and trail sand across the lobby to the bank of elevators.

Curiously enough, neither Rafferty nor Sarah felt a sense of constraint upon reaching their suite. The sudden storm had halted passion, chilling heated flesh and blowing a cold wind through dazed minds, but a part of them remained forever out on a moonlit beach.

He gave her a gentle push toward the other room the moment they were inside the door, trying not to think of how the silk dress clung to her body like a second skin. But it *did* cling, and he *did* think about it, tortured by visions of her naked and passionate; he couldn't shut out the thoughts, but he managed somehow not to act upon them.

"A hot shower, now. You'll catch pneumonia otherwise." Laughing, Sarah disappeared.

She returned to the sitting room less than fifteen minutes later, wearing a thick terry robe, her hair bound up in a towel. "Your turn," she told him, faintly surprised to discover that her shyness had been lost on the beach.

While he was in the shower, Sarah stood before the wide windows looking out at the storm, absently towel-drying her hair. She didn't want to think. Always before in her life, rational thought had crept in to dissuade her from some impulsive action, guarding her from her own folly. But there was something different now, she realized.

She had decided to take that unexplored path, and the interlude on the beach had set her feet firmly on their way. There was, she noted with a sense of relief, no going back now. She felt curiously free, unfettered by the caution and reserve of a lifetime. She had left behind her the woman who had built a wall of shyness and hidden behind it, the woman who had avoided closeness because she felt safer alone.

Hours before she had wanted to strangle Hagen, but now Sarah only wanted to thank him. He had pitchforked her into an uncomfortable situation, forcing her to accept a kind of intimacy with a stranger, and the jolt of that and her instant attraction to Rafferty had been enough to set her free. The passionate interlude on the beach had completed the cure.

She didn't feel familiar to herself, and though that was unsettling, it was also pleasing. She could be anyone, test herself beyond the limits she had come to accept until now.

In a peculiar way—and not consciously recognized by herself—Sarah had only now, belatedly, come of age. She had been pushed by circumstances beyond her control. A personality dampened firmly by rational caution had just received a heady breath of fresh air and freedom, and like any unfamiliar atmosphere, it was rapidly going to her head.

Rafferty found her by the window when he returned from his shower, and he stood gazing at her for a moment. Her tousled hair, still damp, flowed about her head and shoulders in dark gold strands, its natural tendency to wave untamed. The white robe she wore was long, but it parted around a tanned leg as she scuffed her bare toes in the thick carpet, and her slender fingers toyed with the towel she held in front of her.

Rafferty felt his mouth go dry as his eyes watched the terrycloth rise and fall with her breathing, and he knew that neither the sudden storm nor the shower had done anything at all to cool his heated blood. The memory of her instant passion wafted through his mind, torturing him.

He wanted to finish what had begun on the beach, wanted to sweep her off her feet and into the bed in the next room. He wanted to feel her silky legs cradle him, wanted to . . . wanted. He wanted so much to make love to her. Needed to so much . . . but he had no intention of conducting a "shipboard" romance, two strangers meeting on a temporary voyage and indulging in a temporary passion. He could never, he knew, be satisfied with that. He wanted Sarah in his bed, not a stranger who would wave farewell at journey's end with an indifferent smile.

He didn't want a memory.

But when Sarah turned and smiled at him, he fought an impulse to take whatever he could get. Going over to her, he took the towel from her hand and began using it with intentional briskness to dry her hair. "I don't want a sick wife," he told her, pleased by the casual sound of his voice.

Laughing a little, she peered up at him with bright eyes through the damp red-gold tangle. He was wearing slacks and a knit shirt, and though Sarah had no experience in matters such as this, she instantly recognized the signs that Rafferty was more levelheaded than she was at the moment.

Curiously enough, she felt no sense of rejection, and her own reckless enjoyment didn't diminish a bit. If anything, it increased dramatically. She felt aware, sensitized, and the possibilities seemed endless and fascinating to contemplate. And this new Sarah said something that should have surprised the old one. But, somehow, it did not. "Your wife in name only, from the look of it."

If Rafferty hesitated in his task, it was only for a fleeting instant. Lightly, he said, "Restraint is supposed to be good for the soul; I'm trying to build my character. Don't mess it up for me, huh?"

"I wouldn't know how to be a siren," she confessed, unaware that her eyes certainly knew.

Shrewdly, Rafferty said, "But you'd enjoy the opportunity to try?"

A little startled, Sarah realized he was right. She'd gone too far to resurrect shyness, but a faint flush did color her cheeks. "I suppose. I never thought of myself like that." Then she blinked. "Oh, that's ridiculous, Rafferty! With all we have to do . . ."

"I don't know," he murmured. "It might be fun." Mentally, he apologized to a body appalled by the very thought. He was, he knew, inviting torture and sleepless nights. There was much about Sarah Cavell that intrigued him, but seeing that dawn of feminine enjoyment in her eyes fascinated him utterly. Having had no sisters, Rafferty had never watched a woman become aware of her own powers. He had a very strong feeling that he was seeing it now. "You've never gotten involved with a man before, have you?" he asked slowly.

She gave him a hesitant smile. "Well, no. I always thought I was cold-natured."

Rafferty did an exaggerated double take, which sufficed to hide his very real astonishment. Were all the men she had known morons? "I beg your pardon?"

She giggled, flushing again as she remembered her response on the beach. "I did. I just wasn't interested."

"It must have been my charming smile," he said.

Sarah cleared her throat. "Must have been."

"How old are you?" he asked suspiciously.

"Twenty-six."

In mock surprise, he said, "And you've never exercised your feminine wiles? How long has Hagen had you sequestered in that information retrieval office, anyway?"

"Since college." She lifted her chin and met his gaze squarely. "Before that—I told you—I just wasn't interested."

He removed the towel and studied the tangled mass of her hair for a moment, then flopped the towel back over her head. "Find a brush for that," he instructed briskly. "It looks like a rat's nest."

She pushed the towel back, laughing. "Thanks!" But she went and found her brush, lingering in the bedroom long enough to smooth the knots from her hair before returning to the sitting room. As soon as she came back, Rafferty spoke.

"I think it's a good idea."

Sarah lifted a brow at him. "What is?"

"Letting you vamp me."

Three

"Very funny."

"I'm serious." He grinned at her, enjoying her startled expression. "You don't have to start from scratch, you know. Remember the beach? By the time we finish with the assignment, I may well be putty in your hands. I'll even up the ante."

"How?" she asked slowly, staring at him.

Rafferty lifted his hand and brushed her cheek lightly with his knuckles. "Anything you catch," he hesitated, "you keep."

Sarah was smiling before she realized it. Something new within her was rising to the challenge. "Does that line work on all the girls?"

"I wouldn't know. Never used it before. But I think we're both going to enjoy finding out if it works on you."

She crossed her arms beneath her breasts. When his eyes dropped briefly to examine the golden flesh that was bared as the lapels of her robe slid farther apart, she felt a little flicker of warm excitement.

Rafferty cleared his throat carefully. "Let's not start just yet," he murmured a bit hoarsely. "I need a good night's sleep first."

Sarah bit her lip to hold back a sudden giggle. "Let me get this straight. Along with everything else we have to do, we're going to play a game. The game is seduction. And you're the prize?"

Feeling a bit reckless himself, Rafferty grinned. "Something like that. If you don't want me, you can always throw me back, but you have to catch me first." He went to the bar, and fixed them both drinks. Handing one to her, he added gently, "And I intend to play hard to get."

She sipped her drink slowly, her eyes speculative. "Why?" she asked finally.

Rafferty didn't need the question clarified. "Oh . . . because we're going to be in a serious situation and we'll need to take our minds off it occasionally. Because we'll inevitably get to know one another during the process. And because we'll both enjoy it immensely."

"You think so?"

"Don't you?"

Sarah did. Her smile widened. "Are there any rules in this game of yours?"

"Prudence dictates. Nothing blatant. If you took me by the hand and led me in there"—he nodded toward the bedroom—"for instance, that would definitely be blatant. And since I'd feel compelled to defend your honor, don't wear anything that's liable to get you arrested or attacked. Subtlety is our watchword. Otherwise, it's no holds barred."

Fascinated, he watched the speculation grow in her eyes, realizing that he'd willingly torment himself just to see the emergence of a siren. "And I only hope," he muttered, unconsciously completing the thought, "that I'm not creating a monster."

It was a game he was suggesting, Sarah told herself. A stray thought crept into her mind to cause an instant's wavering. Once on Kadeira, his game would be impossible. But that was later. They had time for a game. Just a game. And she didn't think he'd fight too hard not to be caught. She didn't have to be experienced to know that Rafferty quite definitely wanted her. So why not up the stakes to make it more interesting?

That's what she told herself. Just an extra incentive to keep Rafferty from giving in too easily. A heady recklessness seized her, and Sarah heard her own voice emerge with nothing more than faint surprise.

"You upped the ante; now it's my turn."

Looking into her eyes, Rafferty suddenly knew what she was about to suggest. He knew, and surrendered happily to the gleeful fate that had pointed at Sarah and announced, "She's the one!"

"Want to raise the stakes, huh?" He smiled slowly. "All right. I'm game."

"You said that anything I catch, I keep."

"That's right."

"I say, if I catch you, the world has to know about it." She lifted her left hand, where the diamond and the gold wedding band glittered, and her ring finger moved gently.

"A ring and a promise?" he asked.

"No. A ring and a vow. The whole ball of wax."

Rafferty lifted his glass and clinked it against hers. "Deal. You catch me, and we'll make it legal."

A part of Sarah's mind told her that she'd passed reckless minutes ago and had now reached madness. She knew that, but she didn't care. No matter how the game ended, she intended to enjoy it. Her common sense told her no sane man would bet his future as Rafferty had just gambled his, but she didn't really think about that.

The new Sarah didn't want to think at all.

Setting her glass aside, she said gently, "You know, I doubt we'll have separate berths on the *Thespian*. So we might as well get used to sharing a bed, don't you think?"

He glanced through the doorway into the bedroom, then lifted a brow at her. "Testing my fortitude?"

"Well, you certainly can't sleep on the couch, and I refuse to. So it has to be the bed. I prefer the left side, by the way."

"I can make do with the right side," he decided. "Pillow between us?"

"Oh, I think we can trust each other not to hurry the game along. Don't you?"

"Certainly." He said, silently damning his own bright ideas and wondering just how long he could manage not to be caught. He'd be lucky if he lasted the night.

"It's late. I'm going to turn in."

Rafferty watched her go into the bedroom and turn back the covers of the king-size bed. It was then that he discovered he'd definitely been wrong in thinking she wore nothing at all beneath the terry robe. She was dressed all right, as he saw when she removed the robe and tossed it across a chair.

Dressed in a teddy of gleaming peach silk, with a plunging neckline and extraordinary brevity everywhere else. The neckline was edged in lace, thin lace straps alone held the bodice in place, and her golden side showed beautifully through the lace there.

And Rafferty, who had seen quite a bit of seductive sleepwear in his time, watched her slide gracefully into the bed and counted to five before his heart started beating again. Sitting up, she gazed through the doorway at him and lifted a brow questioningly. "Coming?"

He tore his gaze away long enough to look down at his empty glass, then looked back at Sarah alone in the wide and inviting bed. "I think I'll have another drink first," he managed.

"Fine. Good night." She reached to turn out the lamp on her nightstand, then lay back and pulled the covers up to her waist. Turning on her side, she closed her eyes, smiling.

Out in the sitting room, Rafferty fixed himself another drink. Upon reflection, he made it a double.

When Rafferty slid into bed beside Sarah, he

didn't expect to get a bit of sleep; that he slept deeply was entirely due to the fact that he had worked long hours the past week in order to accept this assignment from Hagen. So he slept.

But he dreamed. Green eyes that had been shy and nervous at first glance mocked him gleefully even as they seduced, and he kept reaching for satin skin that somehow eluded him. He felt annoyed at the elusive siren, reaching out again and again to try and draw her close. Then, finally, with a throaty murmur she allowed him to capture her, and he held her tightly.

She was warm at his side, the fragile curves of her body pressed to his. Her hair was silk and his fingers tangled among the strands possessively. His. She was his.

He woke with a start to see daylight brightening the room, and he didn't have to look to see that his dream had become reality. She was snuggled close to his side, one leg thrown across his and her hand lying warmly on his chest.

He gazed down at the spill of bright red-gold hair that was like caged fire, and since the covers had fallen away during the night he could also see just how well the silk teddy fit her petite but richly curved body.

Rafferty knew he should get up—get away from her before he lost his head and lost the damn "game" by default. Instead, he rested his cheek against that bright silky hair and considered the night before. It didn't take his mind off his desire, but it did help.

It occurred to him that between the two of them, he and Hagen had somehow changed Sarah. It had been, he decided thoughtfully, a joint effort. Hagen had pried her loose from her safe world and dumped her in an unfamiliar one, and Rafferty had sparked unfamiliar feelings with his own wild passion, and then issued a challenge. He smiled a little. The result should be interesting—to say the least.

Moving very carefully, he eased away from Sarah's side without waking her and left the bed. He stood there for a moment, gazing down at her. What kind of woman, he wondered, had been jolted to life by this situation? In spite of danger and uncertainty and the fiction of the game they were playing, Rafferty was eager to find out. Everything he felt told him that she was his woman; all that remained was for them to discover just who she was, and if she could feel the same for him.

He dressed and shaved, distracting his mind from thoughts of her by wondering if Hagen's assignment was as simple as it appeared on the surface. Everything he knew of Hagen made him doubt that, yet there was no way to be certain. He was reasonably sure only that he and Sarah would find a few surprises waiting for them in Kadeira.

Finding her still sleeping, he went into the sitting room and closed the door, then made a few phone calls. The first was to Zach, whom he reached on the West Coast and woke out of a sound sleep.

"You're *what?*" Zach asked sleepily.

Rafferty, who liked to admit to folly no more than the next man, sighed and repeated himself. "I said I'm working for Hagen."

More than three thousand miles away, Zachary Steele sat up in his hotel room and rubbed his eyes, then peered out at the blackness of predawn. "Where are you?" he demanded.

"Trinidad. And on Monday I board a yacht called the *Thespian* and set sail for Kadeira."

Zach was silent for a long moment. "I see. My condolences."

Rafferty winced. "Is it that bad down there?"

"It's hell," Zach told him, not mincing words. "No place for Americans—especially when they're rich enough to afford a yacht. I gather that's your role?"

"Something like that."

"What'd Hagen do, blackmail you?"

Rafferty sighed. "Never mind. I know I was a fool. But I'm in this now, and I only have a rough idea of the situation in Kadeira. I need to know as much as possible. Can you find out a little more for me?"

It was Zach's turn to sigh. "Sure. Just give me a few hours."

"I'll call back tonight."

"Hey, be careful, will you?"

"I will. Thanks, Zach."

"Don't mention it."

Rafferty cradled the receiver and sat thinking for a few moments, then made two more calls.

The first was to his law partner to check on the progress of a couple of cases. The second was to Lucas Kendrick.

Sarah woke in the strange bed and sat up abruptly, staring around her at a strange room. It only took her a second to remember where she was, and the muffled sound of a male voice speaking in the next room told her whom she was with. Glancing down, she realized she was on his side of the bed.

Frowning, Sarah rose and began dressing, but her frown faded within moments. Half afraid that the night before might have been only an interlude of insanity, she was relieved to discover that she was still of the same mind, be it sane or *in*sane; she wasn't sure which. In all truth, she had never felt so wonderfully awake and aware, and if there would be regrets later at least she felt none now.

As she brushed her hair, she gazed at herself in the mirror, wondering what had happened to the timid creature who had walked into this hotel. She was gone, it seemed, abandoned like an old skin because the new one had grown in. Whether it would be a fragile new skin or a tough and strong one remained to be seen. Too intrigued by this new version of herself, Sarah still wasn't prepared to question that.

And Rafferty . . .

She turned and headed for the sitting room, anxious to make certain *he* was still of the same mind, and simply eager to see him again. When she opened the door she saw he was on the phone, and she hesitated a moment as his end of the conversation sank into her mind.

"You heard me, Lucas." He was facing away from Sarah, and didn't see her enter the room. "Well, I hope it *isn't* necessary; you know I don't like carrying guns. But, to be on the safe side, I think I'd better. Since you're back in New York, you can find something suitable and ship it down here. Right. Yeah, I will."

The menacing reminder of why they were there should have disturbed Sarah. It didn't. So when he turned away from the phone, she said only, "Is Lucas your partner?"

Rafferty got to his feet slowly, staring at her. "No. No, but he works for Josh Long too. He's a private investigator. Good morning."

"Good morning. You've decided to arm yourself, then?"

"It seemed like a good idea."

"I agree. Hagen said you were a marksman. Where did you pick that up?"

Rafferty was beginning to look a little amused. "You're taking the situation much more calmly today, I see. Any particular reason?"

"I slept on it. Answer the question."

"All right. I shot a man once. By mistake. I meant to frighten him. I didn't want it to happen again, so I learned to use guns. Now I hit what I aim at."

"I see." She looked at him searchingly. "Did the man die?"

"No. He's serving a life sentence. For murder."

"One of the bad guys."

Rafferty grinned, able to look back on that past episode now with rueful humor. "I'll say. He nearly shot me right out from under my white hat."

Sarah smiled at him. "Then you don't regret it. Good. You should never regret things."

"Like challenges issued during a storm?"

"Just like that. You don't, do you?"

"No. Oh, no. In fact, I'm looking forward to the game. I even managed to get a good night's sleep in preparation."

She lifted an eyebrow at him. "That doesn't say much for my powers of seduction."

Rafferty was tempted, but decided not to tell her that she'd nearly awakened in his arms—and would have if he hadn't gotten up first. "That would have been blatant," he told her, injured. "Against the rules."

Sarah suddenly came closer, looking up at him with an innocent air belied by gleaming eyes. "But I have to try to seduce you," she reminded him.

He gazed down at her, thinking that what she was wearing—white slacks and a print blouse—wasn't meant to be seductive, but somehow . . . it seemed to be. "Just tell me something honestly," he said. "Is this an act? Or a part of you even *you've* never seen before?"

"The latter," she murmured, reaching out to fasten a button of his shirt that had come undone. Her hand remained on his chest. "I really don't know where she came from, but I like this Sarah. I think she . . . woke up out on the beach."

Rafferty caught her hand firmly and removed it from his chest. "No seduction before breakfast."

"Another rule?"

"We'll call it that." He sighed, trying to slow his increased pulse and having little luck. "Room service, or d'you want to go out for breakfast?"

"Well, if you're going to be a spoilsport—"

"Out," he decided.

Although that day and the next tried his self-control, Rafferty admitted to himself that he enjoyed the experience. The most drastic change in Sarah had occurred when she'd accepted his challenge; she made no overt effort to seduce him during those first two days. And although her sleepwear continued to be decidedly enticing, and he woke to find her in his arms in the morning, she dressed casually and did nothing so obvious as to walk around their suite half-dressed or ask him to wash her back in the shower.

Yet Rafferty very soon realized that this time he really had fashioned a hell for himself. He knew only too well that this new Sarah was a tenuous emergence, vulnerable even if she didn't realize it. A too rapid resolution of their "game" would send her out of his reach forever; he knew that, knew it with every instinct he could lay claim to. She seemed eager to try her new wings, but any threat of real danger before she got used to those wings would undoubtedly send her flying back to the emotional sanctuary of her caution.

His own desire grew with every hour that passed, and only the fascination of getting to know Sarah even as she got to know herself helped to keep him reasonably in control of his baser urges.

But on Monday, when they stood at the marina gazing out at the yacht *Thespian*, he began to wonder if he should have taken advantage of the privacy behind them. It was obvious they'd have little privacy on the luxurious and expensive yacht. And there was the captain, Siran, a lean, dark man in his thirties with an enigmatic gaze and a strangely dangerous smile. He could have been any nationality, and had a very gentle, polite voice that was like a velvet scabbard hiding a steel blade.

The two men who "assisted" Siran—as *he* put it—were both large, strong men with faces that looked as though they'd encountered unfriendly fists from time to time. They were as alike as bookends, and their names, said Siran with his quick smile, were Tom and Dick. Harry proved to be the cabin "boy." He was all of sixty, with grizzled hair and bright blue eyes, and he assured both Rafferty and Sarah that he was a fine cook, and that they had only to ask for anything they wanted. Anything at all.

Left alone at last in their cabin, they looked around, and both, at the same moment, sighed.

"Did somebody say something about separate berths being unlikely?" Rafferty asked dryly. They stood in the middle of a cabin that was every bit as large as the sitting room in their hotel and the bed they could see in the adjoining cabin was full-size. Sarah looked at him with a smile. "Well, there is only one berth, so to speak. Shall we unpack now, or go up on deck to wave good-bye to Trinidad?"

They heard the muffled sound of engines then, and Rafferty said, "On deck is my choice." As they were making their way topside, he added in a low voice, "Does this yacht belong to the agency? And what about the crew?"

"I have no idea. Want to ask Siran?"

Rafferty glanced in the captain's direction as they moved forward. "Not really."

"It isn't good procedure," she agreed, sitting on a padded bench on the starboard side. "If he *isn't* Hagen's man, we could give the show away. And if he is— Oh, he has to be! We may have to leave Kadeira in a hurry; surely Hagen wouldn't trust a hired captain and crew with this assignment."

"I hope you're right." Rafferty sat beside her, as they both gazed out on the colorful marina. "Judging by what Zach found out, we'll be lucky if we escape Kadeira with our skins, let alone the information."

He had explained all of it to her after he had called Zach back as promised, and Sarah chewed her bottom lip absently as she thought about their situation. She felt Rafferty's gaze on her, but wasn't quite able to straighten out her expression fast enough.

"What is it?" He took her hand, looking at her

her steadily and smiling a little. "What is it that you weren't supposed to tell me?"

The *Thespian* gathered speed as they left the clutter of boats behind, and Sarah drew a deep breath. "I don't think you're going to like it. And I *wanted* to tell you. . . . Hagen told me not to until we reached Kadeira."

"But you're going to tell me now." He knew then that his forebodings about this assignment had been on target. True to character, Hagen had once again decided not to tell everyone everything.

Sarah drew a deep breath. "Actually, it isn't bad. Not really. You see, we probably won't have too much trouble staying in Kadeira as long as we need to. We don't have an invitation, but we do have a kind of special pass."

"Which is?"

"Me."

"Hey!" Lucas Kendrick made a wild grab for something solid to hold onto, only just managing to keep his balance. "Keep both eyes on the road, will you?"

Zachary Steele, whose gaze had not left the clear blue waters of the Caribbean, swung the wheel a bit further to starboard, his own feet planted as solidly as the roots of a great oak. "It isn't my fault you have lousy sea legs," he observed mildly.

Lucas glared at him. "I'm half asleep and suffering jet leg, *not* seasickness," he stated. "If you weren't made of granite, you'd be dead yourself.

You've come three thousand miles further than I have."

"I slept on the plane," Zach said, glancing down to check his heading, then looking back at the water.

Lucas found a reasonably comfortable seat near the wheel, his mind turning to the reasons they were there. "You didn't tell Rafferty we were coming?"

"No."

Gloomily, Lucas said, "The boss is going to murder us. You and I are AWOL, you know."

"Well, no, not really." A faint smile softened Zach's hard face and his gray eyes showed his amusement. "I called Josh. When he'd finished casting aspersions on my ancestors and damning me six ways from Sunday for interrupting his honeymoon, he gave us grudging permission to stick our noses in this."

In a plaintive tone, Lucas asked, "Then why on earth didn't we borrow the yacht instead of renting this damned fishing boat? At least we could have been comfortable."

"And a target," Zach pointed out dryly. "Look, even though no one could trace the registry of the *Corsair* back to Josh, it still reeks of money, and evidence suggests that the government of Kadeira seems to have a fondness for arresting wealthy visitors. Rafferty's already a target in the *Thespian*, but that seems to be Hagen's plan."

Lucas frowned, his strikingly handsome face troubled. "Insane plan, if you ask me. Any idea what's going on?"

"Rafferty didn't say, but I can hazard a few guesses. According to the harbormaster in Trinidad, whom I spoke to before you arrived, the *Thespian* pulled out with its crew and two passengers--Rafferty and a young woman." Zach glanced at Lucas, adding blandly, "his wife, I understand."

"His—?" Lucas mused about that for a moment, then sighed. "Part of the cover?"

"I assume so."

"She's an agent?"

"Again, I assume so. Their destination is Kadeira, which, I discovered, is a political nightmare and believed to be the base for a pretty nasty terrorist organization."

"And Rafferty wanted a gun," Lucas murmured. He was looking grimmer by the moment. "Are we going to storm the place, or hover outside the three-mile limit in case we're needed?"

"Play it by ear. The fishing's supposed to be good near Kadeira, so we'll anchor and keep an eye on the *Thespian*." Zach was frowning, the long scar on his left cheek whitening as always in response to tension. "I'm betting they'll go into port with heaven only knows what kind of plan."

"We need to talk to Rafferty."

"And we will, if we get the chance. But we can't risk blowing his cover. Get your clever mind on that, will you?"

Lucas, who had an inborn talent for stealth and a genuine enjoyment of tactics, grimaced and nodded. But he made a despairing observation, one that both men felt keenly.

"I'm not as devious as Hagen. Who in hell can guess what *he* has in mind?"

"You're going to *what?*" Rafferty asked carefully.

Sarah, who had never in her life been assertive, lifted her chin and met his incredulous gaze calmly. "You heard me. I've seen her, Rafferty, and we could be twins. We even have the same first name. And Andrés Sereno was wild about her; he would have married her in a wedding to rival the British royalty, if she hadn't run away."

"Did it ever occur to you that she might have had good reason to run away from President Sereno?"

"He wasn't cruel to her, or anything like that. Rafferty, he *worshiped* her; he would have given her anything—except her freedom. She had to run away to get that."

"If Hagen told you—"

Sarah smiled. "No. She did. I talked to Sara Marsh two weeks ago. She's hiding because he's got people scattered all over the world looking for her."

Rafferty felt more and more like he was in the middle of a nightmare, and morning was too many long hours away. "And so you're going to take advantage of his obsession with this woman because you could be her twin? Sarah, that man sounds unbalanced! At the very least, he's a *dictator* and used to getting his own way. What if he transfers his obsession to you?"

Softly, she said, "It isn't likely. Still, he'll probably be interested enough to want to spend time with me. We're counting on that."

"Sarah—"

"It's our pass into Kadeira, Rafferty. While I . . . occupy the president, you'll meet with our undercover agent and get the information."

Tightly, Rafferty said, "We're supposed to be married, *newly* married at that. Do I just cheerfully hand over my wife to some obsessed tin-pot dictator? Turn my head while he has his hands all over you?"

She reached out to touch his hand, unsurprised when his only response was a deepening of his stony stare. "Our cover is that we're a newly married couple, with a few problems. We're supposed to stage a public fight or something. And as for his hands being all over me, President Sereno was very gentle with his Sara, Rafferty; he never tried to do anything against her will. In fact, they—they were never lovers."

"Maybe he'll decide to grab what he can this time around," Rafferty suggested. "What then, Sarah? Just how far are you prepared to go in *occupying* him? Did Hagen wave the flag at you and explain that a good agent uses every tool available? Did he suggest a little bit of good old-fashioned whoring to get the job done?"

The question quivered in the air between them.

Sarah drew her hand back as though he'd burned her. She had never looked more poignantly lovely, her green eyes darkened to jade with the hurt.

"Sarah, I didn't mean—"

She got up and moved forward, her slender back stiff. Within minutes she was gone from his sight.

Rafferty stared out over the water, his muscles taut until his body ached. Unforgivable. What he'd said was unforgivable, and not something either of them could forget. And the worst of it was that Rafferty knew it was purely and simply impossible for Sarah to do what he'd suggested. Such a thing was alien to her nature. But he hadn't stopped to *think* at all, he'd just blurted out a hollow accusation born in fear for her and the jealous vision of another man who would be desperate for her love.

And if Andrés Sereno had truly been "wild" about his Sara, then it would probably be inevitable that the man would transfer that emotion to her look-alike. And Sarah would have to cope with that. Sarah, who was so damned vulnerable, so newly awakened that she was like a butterfly fresh from its cocoon, desperately fragile and susceptible to untold damage.

It scared the hell out of Rafferty.

What frightened him most, he asked himself? That Sarah would be hurt somehow while "occupying" the Kadeira president? Or that the charismatic Sereno would fire her awakened senses and capture her heart for his own?

Rafferty knew only too well that his own hold on Sarah was a tentative one. She was attracted to him, perhaps even something more. But she was also aware of the dangers of "shipboard" romances, and Rafferty himself had compounded the problem by proposing to make a game of seduction.

Pretence surrounded them, and pretence was an insidious danger. What would Sarah choose as her reality? Emotions sparked on a moonlit beach with a virtual stranger? Or the adoration of a charming island president? Unusually sheltered and innately shy, would Sarah prefer the golden cage of an extraordinarily powerful and wealthy man's possessiveness to the more normal life that Rafferty could offer?

He was, Rafferty realized, conjuring up horrors. Sarah was here to do a job, to complete an assignment, and he believed that alone would motivate her. Surely she wouldn't be so swept away that she'd forget the ruthless ambition of Sereno *and* his apparent welcome, if not approval, of terrorists in his country. She wouldn't forget that.

Would she?

Slowly, worried and uncertain, Rafferty went in search of her. He passed both Tom and Dick, who were industriously polishing chrome that was already gleaming, and passed Captain Siran, who looked at him for an unreadable instant before smiling briefly and meaninglessly.

Sarah wasn't topside, so Rafferty went below. He found her in their cabin, in the bedroom, where she was busy unpacking. He could read nothing in her delicate face, and it occurred to him then that there was indeed a depth to Sarah even she hadn't plumbed.

"Sarah?"

"Captain Siran says we'll be just outside Kadeira by Wednesday morning," she said, not looking at him. "We won't go in until Thursday, though. Hagen was definite about that."

"Sarah, I'm sorry."

She moved past him to hang several garments in the roomy closet, saying impersonally, "All right."

Rafferty caught her wrist as she tried to pass him again. "Sarah! I didn't mean what I said. I know you'd never—Sarah, it just shook me up, that's all. Sereno could hurt you."

"I'm supposed to be married, remember?" She gazed steadfastly at the third button of his shirt.

"You think he'll care about that? If he wants you, Sarah, a piece of paper and a husband won't stand in his way."

Four

Her face seemed to quiver for just an instant. Tonelessly, she said, "I'm not going to seduce him, Rafferty. I'm just going to distract him long enough for us to get that information. That's my job."

Rafferty realized then that she was scared, that sheer bravado had carried her this far and that precious little of her fragile courage was left now. He reached out, suddenly hating himself for badgering her, but she pulled away stiffly.

"I have to finish unpacking."

He refused to let go of her wrist. "I know I hurt you," he said steadily. "I can never take back what I said, but I didn't mean it. I'm afraid Sereno will hurt you, and I'm afraid of losing you."

Sarah pulled her wrist from his grasp, and this time he didn't try to stop her. She went over to lift a pile of folded lingerie from the suitcase lying open on the bed, then paused to gaze at him with bewildered eyes. "I don't understand you," she said softly. "You talk as if you expect me to be attracted to him. This is a *job*, Rafferty. I don't like anything about it, least of all him. If only half of what's suspected about him is true, the man's a charming monster. Are you so willing to believe I'd crawl into bed with *that?*"

Rafferty went to her quickly, his hands finding her shoulders. "No! No, Sarah."

"Then why? Why do you keep talking as if you do believe it?"

He hesitated for only a moment. "Because . . . you said it yourself, Sarah. You're in an unfamiliar situation, playing an unfamiliar role, and under those circumstances it's hard to hold on to reality. Because if you're really the image of the woman he loved so obsessively, he'll love you the same way—and he *is* a charming man, they say. And because a new Sarah was born on a moonlit beach. I can't help wondering if maybe it *was* the beach, and not me."

Sarah jerked away from him and went to place the armful of silk and lace in a drawer. Then she turned back toward him. "I was afraid of Andrés Sereno until now," she said in a small, still voice. "But I've no need to be afraid of him. He can't hurt me, Rafferty. Not the way you just did."

"Oh, hell, Sarah—"

Her face was white, and her green eyes blazed in a surging tangle of emotions. "It's nice to know what you really think. At least now I know where I stand with you. So *something* started an itch on that beach, and I don't care who the hell scratches it? It was the right time and place, I suppose, and you just happened to be there? Or maybe I got drunk on moonlight, and I'm still a little mad? And anything male with a charming smile is going to sweep me right off my feet?"

"I didn't mean—"

"You did! And you were right when you said we didn't know each other well. We don't know each other at all!"

Rafferty stared at the spot where she had stood, listening to the outer door close with deadly softness. Then he listened to the silence, and his own confused thoughts. He had been so concerned about Sereno taking advantage of Sarah's fragility that he hadn't even considered the fact that he himself could hurt her for exactly the same reason.

"Dammit," he said very quietly.

Sarah stood at the bow, letting the warm wind dry her cheeks and clear her mind. She felt shaken, drained by emotion. The old Sarah, cautious and tentative, suggested that she might have wronged Rafferty, might have read unintended meanings into his words. But this new Sarah, suffering an imperfect control over her emotions, was only too sure she had been right.

He actually *believed* that Sereno, reputed to be charming and charismatic, could—and would—sweep her right off her feet and into his bed! And if not that, then he was half-convinced she had been sent on this assignment under orders to sell herself for the price of stolen information.

Half-convinced she would *take* such orders . . .

Sarah had never in her life felt so wildly furious, so bitterly hurt, and so utterly bewildered. Unaccustomed to extreme highs and lows of emotion, she felt overwhelmed. The battering was too much, just suddenly too much. For the first time in her life, she had taken a chance and risked being hurt, and Rafferty had hurt her deeply. Like a child burned by the heedless touch of a flame, she shied violently from a second experiment.

Using the only defense mechanism left in the confusion of her thoughts, she simply turned everything off.

By the following morning, Rafferty had realized that more than apologies were needed. Sarah had avoided him, and when they were more or less forced to be together—dinner, for instance—she had been utterly silent. And she wasn't giving him the silent treatment, he realized. She simply wasn't *there*.

And when, some hours later, he had left the deck to go to their cabin, Sarah had been in bed and asleep, so far over on her side of the bed she was in danger of falling off.

He hadn't awakened to find her in his arms this time.

Rafferty himself was silent during breakfast, aware that Harry looked at them both anxiously while he served another of his truly excellent meals. But the cabin boy said nothing.

Sarah went up on deck after the meal, and

Rafferty followed. He almost forgot the stone wall between them as he watched her discard her caftan for the astonishingly brief bikini she wore underneath and lie down on a padded lounge. It was a good five minutes—during which he drank in the sight of her curved body—before he reminded himself that Sarah was slipping rapidly beyond his reach.

"We have to talk." He sat down on a matching lounge, forcing his mind away from vivid mental images.

She looked at him, her pale green eyes as enigmatic as seawater, her face immobile. "Do we?"

Rafferty was silent for a moment, not weighing what he was about to say but questioning the timing of it. Not that it mattered; he had no choice. "I read something once—couldn't tell you where, but I believe Virgil wrote it—about falling in love. He remembered the sensation vividly, remembered being swept away by the madness of it. Madness. There's nothing rational about love, Sarah. Nothing predictable. There's just a madness, filled with hopes and fears, literally impossible to control."

Sarah frowned a little. "Just because I look like his Sarah doesn't mean Sereno—"

Softly, Rafferty said, "I wasn't talking about him."

For the first time since she had retreated into herself, Sarah began to feel again. "We don't know each other," she said in a curiously suspended voice.

"Do you think that matters? Do you think it matters that this is the wrong time and place, and Lord knows the wrong circumstances for anything as fragile and unpredictable as love?"

"I don't—"

"Sarah, what I'm trying to tell you is that it doesn't help me to *know* you'd never sleep with Sereno to get that information. It doesn't help to *know* he'd be the last man in the world you could feel an attraction for. It's because love isn't logical or rational that I said what I did yesterday," he finished simply, "because I love you, and I was scared."

She chewed on her lower lip unconsciously, staring at him. And feeling again was painful because the ascent from despair and anger to a giddy, half-frightened happiness was just as abrupt and unsettling as it had been the other way around. And somewhere in that earlier journey, some of the old Sarah had come creeping back in, cautious and wary.

"Rafferty, in a few days, we're both going to be playing parts. A couple on the verge of ending a brief marriage. And I have to try and fascinate a man who'll likely make my skin crawl. You have to meet with an undercover agent and get that information from him." She swallowed hard, wondering what he was thinking behind the glow of his tawny eyes. "In spite of what happened in Trinidad, we can't let our personal feelings control us in this. We can't afford the luxury."

He smiled suddenly. "What am I seeing now? A fusing of two Sarahs? Enough of the new to contemplate vamping an island dictator, and enough of the old to warn me off?"

She managed a faint smile of her own. "That's stating it too simply and you know it."

"Maybe. But it's essentially the truth. And it won't work, Sarah."

"It has to."

He shook his head. "The human element, remember? The scenario you and Hagen have apparently concocted just won't work. I might be able to fake an argument with you; I might even be able to act furious and uncaring for awhile. Maybe a day. And then what? If I come within twenty feet of you and Sereno sees me, he'll know I love you. How will he react to that if you've been busy fascinating him?"

Sarah felt a sudden chill. There were, she realized belatedly, many holes in Hagen's scenario. Although, to be fair, he hadn't planned on "the human element" interfering this time.

Dryly, Rafferty said, "Now you see it. At best Sereno might try to talk you into divorcing me. At worst, he could decide to eliminate one bothersome husband."

The thought of something happening to Rafferty brought her heart up into her throat, and Sarah swallowed hard. "No. No, I won't let that happen. I'll make certain he knows that—that I love my husband. I won't try to fascinate him, I'll just sympathize because he lost *his* Sara. I'll cry on his shoulder. If he knows I love you, he won't hurt you. He won't."

Rafferty was watching her, curiously still. After a tiny pause, he said, "No. Perhaps he won't. I think any man would act against his own nature for you, Sarah."

"I'm ordinary." She looked out over the water,

very conscious of what still hung in the air between them. He had said he loved her, and she had said nothing. She couldn't think, and what she felt was too new and violent to be channeled sanely.

He moved suddenly, sitting on her lounge with a hand on either side of her hips. "Ordinary? If you were ordinary, Sarah, you wouldn't be here. And I wouldn't be here asking if it matters at all that I love you."

She looked at him finally, trying desperately to cope with the wild recklessness of what she felt. "Don't. We can't—I can't let myself—"

Rafferty swore softly and his eyes glittered. "I can't be kind, Sarah. I can't promise to give you time. I can't afford *that* luxury. If I know you care, know there's a chance for us, then maybe I can play my part in all this. But I have to know that."

Sarah didn't know what she would have said then, and was grateful they were interrupted.

"Excuse me," Captain Siran murmured silkily.

Rafferty looked at him, a hard look that didn't invite him to linger. "What is it?"

"We are ahead of schedule," Siran said in a precise tone. "I therefore took the liberty of changing course slightly. There is a small uninhabited island just ahead. Perhaps you would care to go ashore for a few hours? The lagoon is perfectly safe for swimming, and it is a lovely island."

"All right," Rafferty told him. He looked down at Sarah as the captain left them alone again. "I'll go down and have Harry fix us a lunch while I'm changing." His gaze skimmed her bikini. "You're . . . just fine as you are."

Sarah remained where she was for a few minutes after he went below, then got up and slowly pulled on her caftan. She had sunglasses, lotion, and a few other things in a colorful straw beach bag on deck, and she picked it up absently.

Hours alone with a handsome man on a deserted island—the stuff of real romance.

She moved to the railing and watched the small dot of green grow larger as they neared, only half aware that Tom and Dick were preparing to lower the small launch into the water. She had scant time to find an answer for Rafferty, but it wasn't time she needed. She knew the truthful answer.

And she was afraid. Too afraid to let herself believe what she felt. It was true that Rafferty could hurt her far worse than Andrés Sereno ever could. And that was frightening. But what frightened her far worse was the memory of a professional agent who had lost her life and that of her partner because she had dared to love. Because she had taken that chance. And if *she* hadn't been able to cope with the madness of love in the midst of a dangerous assignment . . . what chance had Sarah?

The human element. They hadn't chosen this, but they had to deal with it.

The fatalism born on a moonlit beach crept over Sarah again as she waited for him, and she welcomed it. Of course it wasn't love. She couldn't let it be love. It was passion, and that *could* be dealt with. She closed her mind to thoughts of what lay beyond the island they approached. That other island was still days away.

This was the one that mattered.

Siran watched the launch until it reached the island, then selected a particular channel on the radio and made a call. It was answered promptly.

"Go."

"They are on the island," Siran reported tonelessly. "Their plan is to remain several hours. Over."

"And the other boat? Over."

Siran glanced down at an unusual bank of equipment. "Not visual yet, but I have them on the scope. The boat will see us clearly, but will approach from the other side of the island as projected. Over."

"Do nothing—repeat, nothing—to interfere. When your passengers are aboard again, proceed on course for Kadeira. Report to me again on Thursday morning. Understood? Over."

"Understood. Over and out."

Siran turned off the radio and sat back. Reflectively, he lit a cigarette. Still and silent as a lazy cat, he waited, dark eyes scanning the horizon.

Rafferty watched her swim, his own motions automatic. She had pulled a rubber cap over her beautiful hair and swam with expert ease, but her delicate face held an abstracted expression. For his part, Rafferty used the swimming as exercise badly needed to burn off some of his restless energy.

He knew he had pushed her with his insistent

question on board the yacht, but he also knew he no longer had a choice. Finding out what part Sarah was slated to play in the coming assignment had changed everything. She *was* vulnerable now, and in the fabric of pretence surrounding them, Rafferty had to be certain that she held the same thread of reality as himself.

They were real. What they felt was real.

The reckless fatalism he had recognized in her earlier had posed no threat—then. By proposing a game in which she could have tested herself and the limits of that newfound daring, he had ensured that she would have the time she needed to discover for herself what was real. But that was no longer possible, he thought.

How could he make her understand what he feared? He feared for her because she would be so dangerously close to a man the world called a monster. He feared for her because that man would likely be even more unpredictable where she was concerned. And he feared for her—and himself—because a man with the sheer magnetism of Andrés Sereno could prove a formidable rival. Particularly when the woman both men wanted was enmeshed in a web of falsehood and deceit and imbued with a reckless fatalism.

It didn't matter, Rafferty thought, that Sarah felt distaste for Sereno and his methods. The point was that she had nothing real to hold on to. Even her own emotions and reactions were unfamiliar to her, and heaven knew the situation facing them threatened to produce the kind of tension and anxiety that was virtually guaranteed to batter certainty about *anything*.

Rafferty followed her with his gaze, trying to decide what to do, trying to ignore the effect her black bikini was having on his senses. Not that he could.

They had been silent all the way to the island, and she had gone into the lagoon to swim without a word. He watched her, and thought: What will be, will be.

Rafferty followed her at last to the wide strip of white beach. He was aware that he was no nearer to solving the problem. He had the faintest flicker of an idea, but didn't know if it would work; still, he had to try. He had no choice. If there was time . . . perhaps. If there was in Sarah some deeply buried stubbornness, some reluctance to surrender herself totally to a destiny uncontrolled by herself.

Perhaps.

They had drawn the launch into shallow water in the lagoon and tied it to a twisted palm, and they'd spread out a blanket on the sand. It was a secluded spot; they couldn't see the yacht because the mouth of the lagoon was narrow and virtually hid the open sea beyond. And the island was quiet, with only a soft breeze rustling the palms and the faint twittering of birds to be heard.

Rafferty dried off with one of the towels they'd brought along, watching while she did the same. It was cooler here, shaded, and Sarah had pulled on her caftan after releasing her hair from the swim cap. He shrugged into a pale green shirt, but left it unbuttoned.

They were sitting on opposite corners of the

large blanket, and he felt wryly amused for a brief moment. But only for a moment. "Anything to drink?" he asked finally.

Sarah opened the basket Harry had sent along. She gazed at the contents, then said unevenly, "Harry's a romantic; he sent wine for lunch. However . . ." She reached in and withdrew two cans, handing one to Rafferty. "Soft drinks too."

Rafferty took a swallow of his drink, mentally and physically bracing himself. "You've had time. *Does* it matter at all that I love you?"

"Of course it matters." She was staring at her drink, then she lifted shy eyes to meet his.

"How does it matter?" He deliberately kept his voice impersonal, forcing all his thoughts to focus on what he was trying to do. To let nothing else distract his mind. During his work in the criminal courts he had learned to do just that, to concentrate all his energies on the intent to pull a desired response from a witness. Sometimes it worked.

"It matters . . . because I know you—you believe that."

"That's all?"

She made a helpless gesture, beginning to look troubled and unsure. "All? No, it's not all. You know very well I'm not—not indifferent."

He laughed shortly, forcing the sound out and keeping his eyes coolly focused on her.

Her chin lifted at his derisive laughter. "All right, then! I want you, Rafferty—is that what you want to hear? You know it's true. We'd be—we'd be lovers now if you hadn't proposed that little game."

"Forget the game," he said in a hard tone. "That fell apart when Sereno entered the picture. You can hardly try to seduce me while convincing him you're on the fine edge of being available, now can you?"

"I said I wouldn't—"

"We're here alone together on a deserted island," he went on as if he hadn't heard her, his voice deliberately stony. "Nice timing, huh? We've got the whole day. No one to bother us. No one to interrupt. And we want each other."

Her eyes were filling with tears, her delicate face revealing how bewildered she felt. And Rafferty hated what he was doing. But he gritted his teeth and forged ahead, gambling his future on the instinct telling him this would work if anything would.

"You said you wanted to take full advantage of the voyage, remember, Sarah? You also said it was me that changed things on that beach, and not a full moon and a strip of sand. Not just an itch anybody could scratch, remember? Well, since we're fated to work our way through this passion of ours, maybe we'd better start."

"I don't understand—"

"Oh, I think you do."

Sarah tried to draw a breath, discovering it did nothing to slow the panicked thumping of her heart. All during their swim, she had been conscious of excitement, stealing glances at him but finding his own lean face preoccupied. Still, she had expected Rafferty to follow up on the declaration he'd made on the yacht. And she had been prepared to abandon herself, to let these fateful hours alone with him carry her where they would.

But Rafferty wasn't the same man somehow. His handsome face was impassive, his voice all but indifferent. He spoke of love and passion in an utterly matter-of-fact manner, as if those emotions were simply knotty problems to be dealt with in order to get on with more important matters.

But Sarah was remembering a moonlit beach and glittering tawny eyes, and her body was heavy and tingling. If he had reached for her, held her, she would have forgotten everything but him. This implacable "discussion" shocked and confused her, and her body's reaction to him made the rest all the more bewildering.

She got to her feet shakily, hardly aware of setting her soda aside, watching as he did the same and rose to regard her with shuttered eyes.

"What are you saying?" she managed at last.

He lifted an eyebrow at her, the perfect expression of polite disbelief altering his face for an instant. "It has to be spelled out? All right. What I'm saying, Sarah, is that since you aren't prepared to fight fate, we might as well begin this passionate affair of ours. That is what you expect, isn't it? A shipboard romance, over at journey's end? You've never for one moment believed there could be more than that between us."

"Rafferty—"

"I tell you that I love you, and you're completely convinced that I mean it—*for the duration.* Fine. If I have to say good-bye when this is over, I at least want a memory. And since the remainder of this voyage promises to be a bit cluttered for you, it looks like this is my best chance. Oh, you don't have to worry," he went on casually. "I won't be a problem for you. Unrequited love is so boring, isn't it? I'll just count this madness of mine as a learning experience. Next time I'll make certain I don't fall in love at the wrong time."

Panic was still rising, and Sarah had the peculiar feeling that a stranger confronted her. A frightening stranger. And when he reached for her, his face still impassive, panic choked her. This wasn't—this wasn't *right!* She couldn't do this, couldn't let her body's reaction to him fling her into a cold-blooded affair meant to last only until . . .

"No!" She backed away from him, her denial choked, her face white and dazed. "No, I can't—you said you loved me."

"But that doesn't matter to you," he said remorselessly. "You don't really believe it. So it isn't important, is it? The only thing that's important is this attraction we feel. We were destined to be lovers, Sarah, you know that. And there's no use fighting fate, is there?"

Baffled, hurt, Sarah tried to make sense of what she was feeling. Her recklessness surged, along with the willingness to be carried away on a tide of emotion. And in that moment the fusion Rafferty had relentlessly striven for took place.

The heedless abandon born on a moonlit beach collided violently with a lifelong caution and prudence, and the vastly different traits merged simply because they could coexist no other way. A transition that should have been gradual was forced, hurriedly and painfully, leaving Sarah shaken and curiously numb.

She wasn't aware that she was crying at first, feeling only a dim grief for the giddy, brief freedom of recklessness. Then she realized that Rafferty was holding her, that he had picked her up and then sat down to cradle her on his lap, and that he too was shaking.

"I'm sorry," he was murmuring unsteadily into her hair. "I didn't want to hurt you. I never want to hurt you."

"Why—?" she whispered, wondering why she didn't blame him for the distant pain.

He held her closer, tighter. "Darling, I don't want you to say yes because you feel powerless to fight this. I can't *let* you feel that way, because you're going into a situation where it could destroy you." His voice was low, intense. "Destroy us both." He drew a deep breath. "Lord knows I want us to be lovers, but it's because I love you. I don't want just a memory, and I'll fight like hell to make certain I'm not left with only that."

He tilted her face up and kissed her gently, his eyes as shadowed as her own. "A good friend taught me a lot about control," he told her soberly. "He controlled obsessively, and it nearly destroyed him. But there's a middle ground, Sarah, and that's where we have to stand. If we let ourselves be powerless, we're asking to be carried along on someone else's tide. We have to fight to discover what's real, and what we really want."

She gazed at him, wondering at the change in

his expression. No longer impassive, his eyes no longer shuttered, he was looking at her now with a face haggard with emotion and eyes that held pain and remorse and driven determination. She swallowed the lump in her throat, grappling with what he was telling her, understanding even before she consciously realized it.

"You did that deliberately. You wanted me to be responsible. To decide."

He brushed a strand of red-gold hair away from her face, his lips tightening briefly as if in anguish. "I had to. Because if you once let yourself be swept away without fighting, Sarah, it'd be easier to give in next time. Easier to just take the simple way, the reckless way. And that wouldn't have hurt you with me, because I'd wait until you finally faced it, and I'd do my damnedest to help you through it. But if you *did* take the easy way with me now, there'd be no time for that. No time to work through it. Because you have to deal with Sereno so quickly, and he *won't* wait."

She stiffened and started to pull away, but Rafferty held her firmly, and his voice was flat.

"We're not talking about sex, Sarah. We're talking about emotions. And if you don't think you can fight me—how you feel with me—then how could you possibly think you'd be able to fight *him?*"

Hovering on the edge of anger, Sarah was drawn back by the sudden understanding of what he meant. He wasn't accusing her of having no moral standards, nor was he implying that she was so sexually susceptible even a charming animal could get her into his bed. What he was saying was that if she allowed herself to remain passive in a man's arms *once* . . . then it would be the easiest thing in the world for that to happen again.

Appalled at the realization, she asked a little breathlessly, "Are you telling me to fight you?"

"Yes." His response was instant. "I don't *want* to sweep you off your feet, Sarah. I don't want a blind lover. I want you to *know* what making love with me will mean. Not an affair, not a shipboard romance, and not a fling because we've been thrown together in an impossible situation and it's easier to give in rather than understand."

Sarah's eyes widened. "That's what—I was afraid it'd happen to us. Afraid that if my mind was involved, I'd somehow get us killed when there was danger. I thought if—if we were lovers without being in love . . ."

Rafferty remembered her agent friend, and understood. He nodded slowly. You wanted to be swept away, because you'd convinced yourself that if it was only passion, there was no danger. You weren't afraid ours would be a passing affair, Sarah. You *wanted* it to be just that. Nothing dangerous. Nothing threatening. We'd part when it was over . . . but we'd both be alive. That's it, isn't it?"

"I think it is," she whispered, staring at him. "Rafferty . . . I'm sorry." She buried her face in his neck, her arms slipping inside his shirt to hold him.

His arms tightened, and his voice was husky. "I'm just glad you realize that now. Sarah? I do love you."

Because she knew he was waiting, she looked at him finally, and felt her heart turn over. "I—thought I was feeling so much before, but I wasn't letting myself feel at all." But now she was feeling, and it was in her eyes.

"Sarah . . ." His head bent, slowly, and his lips found hers. For an instant he was gentle, tentative, but then the ragged emotions of the past hour overwhelmed restraint and his mouth slanted across hers, deepening the touch.

He could feel her melt against him instantly, her hands sliding over his back, her mouth opening to him in a surging response. Through the thin silklike material of her caftan he could feel the heat of her flesh, and he moved without even thinking about it, lifting her, placing her on the blanket and lying next to her.

They had shared a bed. They had shared a burst of flame on a moonlit beach and agreed on a lighthearted game to cope with the fire. They had weathered the first deceit, each believing the other beyond reach. They had laughed together and argued. They had spent this interlude on a deserted island tautly stripping away pretence and illusion. They had even been cruel to each other.

And for the first time, they were truly themselves together, vulnerable, still not quite certain what had burst into life between them and still not quite certain how to cope.

Sarah had been told to fight, but that was beyond her at the moment. At the same time, she was no longer being carried blindly away by desire; she knew very well what was happening. Her body was responding in a fiery urgency to the man holding her, kissing her, and what she was feeling was more than passion.

She didn't want to fight that.

Rafferty kissed her as if he were starving for her, and her response only deepened the hunger. He explored the warmth of her mouth, his tongue possessing starkly. One hand tangled in the silk of her hair while the other slid down along her side, and the slight friction of thin material between his flesh and hers reminded them both of maddening barriers.

Sarah couldn't breathe even when his lips left hers to trail down her neck; she tilted her head mindlessly, her hands stroking his back, probing strong muscles that were hard with tension. For the second time an interlude on a beach was awakening astonishing feelings in her body and mind, but this time she was not conscious of the risk in taking an unexplored road; being with Rafferty was the most natural, inevitable thing in the world.

"Dammit, fight me," he murmured against her ear, and there was a strained thread of humor in his deep voice.

She smiled when he lifted his head to gaze down at her, unaware that her own eyes were darkened like his, dazed like his. "I don't want to fight you," she said huskily.

"You're so beautiful," he told her in a thickened voice. "And I want you so much. . . . For heaven's sake, tell me to stop, tell me you need time to think things through. . . ."

"You changed the rules on me," she complained. "*You* were supposed to fight *me* off, remember?"

"Somebody else changed the rules." He kissed her briefly, hard. "Damn Hagen!"

Uninterested in anyone else at the moment, Sarah brushed her fingers up his spine slowly, glorying in his instant response. "What would you say . . . if I said I didn't need time to think things through?"

Rafferty half closed his eyes, his expression midway between pain and pleasure. "I'd say it's too soon. You have to be sure, Sarah."

"We'll be in Kadeira soon," she reminded him softly.

He sighed a bit raggedly, his eyes flaring at her. "I know. Still, we have a little time."

"Rafferty—"

"Excuse me?"

The sound was a shock, since it was a third voice on an island supposedly containing only two people. And the fact that the voice, while deep and utterly male, was also soft and effortless did nothing to cushion the blow. The shock factor on a scale of ten was several points over the top.

After the first second Rafferty turned his head slowly. His face was frozen with astonishment. "I don't believe it," he murmured.

Five

"This is becoming a habit," Zachary Steele commented about a minute later. "It's the second time in a couple of months I've had to interrupt a pair of lovers at what I judge to be a critical moment."

Rafferty and Sarah had disentangled themselves and were sitting side by side on the blanket, both gazing at their visitor. They were too bemused to be embarrassed, and the abrupt end to their interlude alone had left them feeling somewhat suspended.

Sarah, who had recognized Zach's name when he'd politely introduced himself, studied him with surprise. She didn't know what mental image had formed when Rafferty had described this friend, but his appearance was rather startling. He was big, for one thing—four or five inches over six feet—and built to fill doorways. He was a potentially dangerous man, she thought, despite the almost bland expression on his rugged face and his serene gray eyes. And the long narrow scar on his left cheek hinted at dangerous things he'd done in the past. Wearing only swim trunks, he exuded a peculiarly animal vitality, every inch of tanned flesh covering corded muscle; the smooth expanse of bronze was broken only by the jet-black hair covering his chest and lightly furring his long powerful legs.

In a detached manner, Sarah thought that most women would find him utterly riveting physically and curiously fascinating otherwise; he was unquestionably masculine from head to toe. If they'd met on a street corner, she didn't doubt he would have frightened her, but here on a tropical island and seeing that special gleam of amusement in his eyes, she decided she liked him very much.

"Oh, good, lunch!"

Amazed, Sarah looked up at their second visitor, who had emerged from somewhere behind Zach and was now cheerfully exploring the picnic basket. She barely heard Rafferty sputtering beside her.

This, she decided, would have to be Lucas Kendrick, Rafferty's other friend. The investigator. He, too, was a big man, a bit over six feet and broad-shouldered, with the beautifully defined muscles of a very active man. He was also strikingly handsome, with classical features and a leonine mane of silvery blond hair. That hair, Sarah decided thoughtfully, could easily inspire a woman to want to run barefoot through it. And if he didn't exude quite the raw force of Zach or the keen intelligence of Rafferty, he could certainly talk the devil out of hell with that charming voice.

Sarah was mildly pleased with herself because these two men aroused no more than a spark of interest and a detached curiosity in her. Attractive though they undoubtedly were, she would have instantly traded them and every other man she'd ever met for Rafferty.

Andrés Sereno, I'm ready for you! she thought in satisfaction.

"What the hell," Rafferty was asking coldly, "are you two doing here?"

Lucas took it upon himself to answer, elaborately casual and still looking through the basket. "Oh, we were in the neighborhood. Just passing by. Would you look at this spread? That boat of yours must have some chef."

Rafferty turned his stony gaze to Zach, who had settled himself on the blanket and now returned Rafferty's stare blandly. And it occurred to Sarah that both visitors shared a healthy respect for Rafferty, and that each was somewhat wary at the moment, despite calm expressions and casual words.

These men, she thought, were certain of what she had sensed in Rafferty: that understated power of his. She made a mental note to discover more about their friendship. Apparently, it had weathered a few storms.

Infinitely patient, Rafferty said, "Just passing by, huh? Passing by a supposedly deserted island in the Caribbean? How far'd you have to swim to just pass by?" He looked pointedly at the wet trunks both men were wearing.

"Our boat's anchored offshore," Zach told him. "On the other side of the island. Don't worry, I doubt your skipper saw us. And if he did, we're just fishermen."

A little fiercely, Rafferty said, "*You* are supposed to be in California." He turned his stare on Lucas, adding, "And *you* in New York. Who the hell's minding the store?"

"By now, Josh," Zach answered. "He got tired of people interrupting his honeymoon and said he might as well come home."

That surprised a laugh out of Rafferty, but he was almost instantly grim again. "Now I know how he felt when we butted into *his* business. Look guys, go home."

"And miss the opportunity to fish off the shores of Kadeira?" Lucas asked, his tone ironic.

Sarah giggled, but hastily straightened her face when Rafferty gave her an offended glance. She was enjoying this immensely, and had the sneaking suspicion that Rafferty wasn't quite as angry as he seemed. From the sound of it, these three made it a habit to watch out for one another, and she liked that. Their kind of friendship was rare in her experience.

Still striving for patience, Rafferty told his friends, "You've both helped enough. Besides, this is a difficult situation. You two can't possibly get into Kadeira without attracting just the kind of attention we're trying to avoid."

"You couldn't pass for a native," Zach observed. "Neither could Sarah."

Hearing her name, Lucas looked up long enough

to charmingly introduce himself. Sarah responded gravely, trying not to laugh in the face of Rafferty's comical despair.

"Hagen arranged—"

"Oh, *Hagen* did," Zach said in a surprised but somehow odd tone, as if he were implying something.

Rafferty gritted his teeth. "All right, so he's sneaky as hell and prone to keep certain things to himself. I *know* that. And I'm none too happy about this scheme, but—" He glanced at Sarah, then swore under his breath.

He wouldn't tell them, Sarah realized, because it was her assignment too. So she told them, trusting them because he did, and because she liked them. She told them the plan, explaining everything—except one tiny detail even Rafferty didn't know yet, and which she couldn't tell him until they were on the island.

She told herself that it was hardly professional to disclose so many particulars of their assignment—let alone to strangers—but she was following instinct. She was also half-consciously rebelling against Hagen's secretive orders, plans, and general disposition.

Zach looked at her, then at Lucas, who had also listened intently to the story. "That seems to let us out," he commented.

The blond man made a faint grimace of agreement. "Seems to. Too many nosy Americans on the island could gum up the works nicely, I'd say."

"Let's have lunch," Zach suggested.

Rafferty regarded him suspiciously, and it was Sarah who responded. "Harry packed enough."

She measured Zach's huge frame with a musing gaze, adding, "I think."

Zach's smile was surprisingly gentle. "Oh, I don't eat much."

Lucas, who was examining the bottle of wine with a critical eye, did an exaggerated double take and stared at the big man incredulously. "You don't what?"

"Luc, would you care to swim to the nearest country that'll have you?"

"He eats like a bird," Lucas told Sarah somewhat hastily.

Sarah was trying not to giggle, and Rafferty seemed resigned to the situation. But he wasn't nearly as glum as he appeared, because he winked at Sarah when neither of the other two was looking.

Lunch was enjoyable, even though there weren't enough plates or glasses to go around, and Zach and Lucas took turns drinking from the wine bottle. Sarah was fascinated by the friendship of the three men. They were utterly comfortable with each other, and with her, and though rude remarks and cheerful insults seemed the order of the day, there was also an obvious closeness among them.

And there was, she learned not entirely to her surprise, a fourth friend present in spirit.

"Is Josh really back at the helm?" Rafferty asked the other two.

"He got in touch this morning," Zach affirmed. "Told us very politely that since we'd all decided to be idiots, he thought he should come home."

"Heard Raven laughing in the background," Lucas added.

Rafferty frowned a little. "Wait a minute. Got in touch *how?*"

Zach was intently studying what remained of a drumstick. "By radio," he murmured.

Sarah, startled, said, "But then he'd have to be—"

"Not in the South Pacific," Rafferty said. "And not in New York. Don't tell me—"

Lucas was grinning a little. "The *Corsair* we think. His own yacht. And since Zach wired that boat, anybody could run anything from it. So, Josh *is* minding the store. By remote control."

"Where is he?"

"He wouldn't say," Zach replied. "My guess is that he's somewhere here in the Caribbean. But he knows the situation on Kadeira, Rafferty, and he won't get anywhere near the place. He's just standing by."

"In case I get into trouble," Rafferty muttered.

"In case any of us do. He'll call out the troops if something goes wrong. And we all know that when Josh calls out the troops, things happen. Hell, he even knows Sereno personally."

Both Rafferty and Sarah blinked. "He does?" she asked.

"He does. The guy wanted businessmen to invest in his country a few years ago, just after he came to power, and Josh was at the top of his list. That was when the political situation on Kadeira was better—relatively speaking, of course."

"Josh actually met with him?" Rafferty asked, clearly surprised.

"Yeah. You were over in Europe straightening out something for Rena—Josh's sister," he explained in an aside to Sarah. "Sereno was in New York. He called and asked for an appointment. Then he came to the office, and not thirty minutes later Josh cancelled his appointments for the rest of the afternoon. Sereno and Josh spent hours talking."

Still incredulous, Rafferty said, "Now there's something I wouldn't have believed. Josh is so rabid against anyone with that brand of ruthlessness. And even then Sereno was known for his ruthlessness. I'm amazed he met with Sereno at all, much less spent hours talking to him."

Zach looked at him thoughtfully. "Josh sent a message to you, by the way. Said you should keep it in mind while dealing with Sereno."

"What?"

" 'Shades of gray.' "

The *Thespian* got underway just before dusk, and Rafferty and Sarah remained on deck to watch the fiery sunset. The atmosphere between them was both better and worse than it had been before their trip to the little island. It was better because they had cleared up some of the tensions resulting from their situation, and worse for the same reason.

The clock was ticking away their private moments together.

"Shades of gray," Sarah mused, standing beside Rafferty as they gazed out on blue water touched with crimson. "Did he mean what I think he meant?"

Rafferty, too, was troubled by that cryptic message. "That a man painted black still has shades of gray in his character? I can't think of another meaning. I *know* Josh, and he wouldn't have spent any time at all with Sereno unless there was something positive in the man. Something redeeming."

Sarah looked at him curiously. "*Would* he have known? I mean, is he that perceptive?"

"Josh? Oh, yes. He's a world-mover, Sarah; he's dealt with powerful men most of his life. And he's a prime target for every sort of con, every kind of sob story you could name. People have always tried to win him over for one reason or another—mostly financial ones. If he met with Sereno at all, it was because he was willing to listen. And the fact that he *did* listen for hours tells me that it was a difficult decision for him to make. He didn't invest in Kadeira, but he had to think it over carefully before he decided not to."

"I wonder if Sereno's bitter about that."

"Who knows."

She thought awhile, thought about complex men and world movers. Then she looked at Rafferty and smiled. "Tell me something?"

"Sure."

"In your work, you've faced off against both male and female attorneys in court. Right?"

"Of course." He looked at her curiously.

"Would I be right in assuming that you usually win against men, and usually lose against women?"

Rafferty was obviously startled. "Well, yes, as a

matter of fact. I've never been able to figure it out. Honestly speaking, I've won against male attorneys I knew were better lawyers, and lost to women I knew weren't particularly strong. I assume you mean *won* in the sense of courtroom tactics, where a case depended more on the presentation of facts rather than the facts themselves?"

"That's what I mean." She laughed a little when he lifted a questioning brow. "Yes, I think I know why."

"Why, then? I've always wondered. I don't *think* I treat a female opponent any differently."

"No, probably not. But I'll bet they treat you differently, Rafferty."

"In what way?"

"They don't underestimate you."

For a brief moment, there was a curious gleam in the depths of his golden eyes. Then it was gone, and he slid his arms around her to pull her close. "Ah. And do you underestimate me?"

Her hands crept beneath his unbuttoned shirt until the warm flesh of his back was smooth beneath her palms. "I hope not," she murmured. "Underestimating you would be very dangerous, I think."

His arms tightened, and Rafferty's eyes focused on her mouth. When he spoke, his voice was husky. "One of these days, you'll have to explain that to me."

Drawn inexorably by those topaz eyes, Sarah had begun to move up on tiptoe to be even closer to him when her peripheral vision caught sight of Tom or Dick—she could never tell which was which—moving past them with an armful of ropes. She drew back a step.

Rafferty had seen him as well. "Damn. When this is over, you and I are going someplace where we can be alone." He lifted a hand to stroke her cheek. "Really alone."

Sarah rubbed her cheek against his warm, rough palm, feeling very conscious of both their lack of privacy and the heavy ache deep inside her. She wanted him. And there was no hiding or disguising that hunger when she looked at him.

He caught his breath, and the last rays of the setting sun painted his lean face with a hot reddish light. For a timeless moment he did indeed look dangerous, his features carved out of fire and his eyes ablaze. There was a hardness in his face, a driven strength. There was something primitive and savage.

She watched the transformation, as one would watch the rippling of subtle muscles beneath the gleaming skin of a caged tiger, with wonder and fascination but no fear. It was not a trick of light, she thought dimly, but something else, some momentary revelation of what lay beneath his civilized exterior. He had hidden that part of himself, and she wondered why it had escaped now, never realizing that she had looked at him with naked hunger for the first time.

The hand against her cheek trembled slightly even as the last of the sunlight vanished, and Rafferty's face was his own again. Almost his own. There had been a subtle alteration during the moment of blazing light, leaving that inner core of him nearer the surface, more exposed. The deceptive layer of easygoing softness seemed to have been partially stripped away, and he was visibly more powerful, stronger, tougher.

She wondered, vaguely, if men would underestimate him now.

She didn't think so.

"Sarah . . ." He drew a ragged breath, as if his lungs were starved for air, and in the deepening twilight it was easy to see he was shaken. "Don't look at me like that."

"Like what?" she murmured, still fascinated by him.

Hoarsely, he said, "Like we're in bed together with nothing between us."

After a moment, she slowly moved back away from him. It was not a rejection, or even a denial of his words. She was smiling a little, unconsciously sensual. "I think I'll go—wash away the sand and salt."

He swallowed. "I'll be along later."

Rafferty moved slowly to the bow, welcoming the cool, brisk wind on his face. His entire body was throbbing, slowly and heavily, and he stared at the darkening horizon without really seeing it.

There were a hundred things he should have been thinking of. The coming poker game with Sereno, danger, the presence of his friends, Josh's cryptic message. But what he thought of was Sarah, and the question branded in his mind was whether the interlude on the island had truly freed her, strengthened her.

Gripping the chrome railing, Rafferty acknowledged to himself that the answer to that question made little difference now. It was clear she wouldn't "fight" him, wouldn't resist the passion between them. Only time would tell if that decision was wise, and the right one. Only time would tell if Sarah was indeed in control of her destiny.

Rafferty didn't know how long he stood in the cooling wind, but at the same moment he became aware of darkness and of a presence at his side. And he tensed, an instinctive recognition of power, feeling physically what he had only sensed before now.

"Mr. Lewis?"

Danger. Siran was dangerous. In the darkness especially, he was dangerous. "Yes?"

"Harry asked that I tell you dinner is served."

"Thank you, Captain." Rafferty felt rather than saw Siran vanish, and he was both elated and bothered by that. Elated because this newfound instinct boded well for the coming foray into Kadeira. And bothered because he didn't know what had unleashed it. He knew only that he had never felt so aware, so acutely sensitive to his surroundings.

Rafferty made his way below deck and into their cabin, surprised to find the lighting dim and the room apparently deserted. And then she spoke, from the shadows.

"Harry's serving dinner in a few minutes; I told him you'd probably want to take a shower first."

"You were right." He cleared his throat, not seeing her clearly, but very aware of her presence. She was still and silent now. After a brief hesitation, he headed for the shower.

When he returned to the main cabin, wearing slacks and a white shirt with the sleeves rolled up over his forearms, he found a table set for two, the dishes under silver covers and wine chilling on ice. Harry was absent, and when Sarah came forward and into the faint light, Rafferty realized that she had planned this.

"Pushy lady," he murmured, but his gaze was moving over her hotly. Obviously, Sarah had decided that subtlety was a waste of time. Her hair, falling loosely over her shoulders, gleamed richly, and her creamy skin was a perfect foil for the stark black creation she had chosen to wear.

The negligee was silk, shimmering in the half-light. The sleeves were long and full, caught tightly at her wrists, and they were fashioned of lace that allowed the warmth of her flesh to show. The negligee fell straight from her shoulders to the floor, and beneath it her gown boasted a deep V-neck and was gathered tightly beneath her breasts. Her every movement caused the thin fabric to mold itself against her, outlining the delicate curves of her hips and thighs.

"We were interrupted on the island," she said softly, her eyes glowing with the mystery of a cat's. "But not tonight. Harry has his orders."

Rafferty glanced at the table awaiting them, and he knew he'd never force food past the tightness of his throat. He looked back at her, watching her as she moved closer, and he could hardly breathe. But he managed a last reluctant, automatic protest.

"This is—definitely blatant."

Sarah halted barely an arm's length from him,

smiling. "No more rules," she reminded him. "You stopped that game, remember? So you have nothing to lose."

Rafferty tried to think of practicalities. "Sarah, I can't protect you. I just haven't been thinking—"

Her eyes softened even more. "Don't worry. It's a requirement for female agents on field assignments. He might not know much about the human element, but Hagen does anticipate some human failings."

Not even conscious of moving, Rafferty watched as his hands came to rest on her shoulders, feeling the silk and the warm flesh beneath. "I love you," he murmured huskily as the last thread of his willpower snapped.

They stood as they were for an eternal moment, as if each was giving the other a last opportunity to draw back, to stop before anything irrevocable happened. But neither drew back. Instead, Sarah stepped closer, lifting her face, long dark lashes shadowing her gleaming eyes. Rafferty's head bent, and his lips touched hers. At first his kiss was a whisper, a gently, tentative caress, but that wasn't enough for either of them.

Sarah felt his fingers tighten, and her own hands lifted to slide around his waist. The heavy ache inside her intensified, spreading throughout her body, and she pressed against him suddenly in an attempt to ease that hurt. Her mouth opened to the fierce demand of his, and all her senses whirled at the thrusting possession of his tongue.

What she felt was still new to her, wonderfully unfamiliar, yet Sarah recognized what was born in her then, and accepted the inescapable, overpowering need to belong to him. There was no future, no past, there was only this night. And it was not fatalism that bred her need, but rather something far deeper and utterly feminine.

His hands slid down her back and to her hips, shaping the rounded flesh and pulling her closer, until she could feel the swelling demand of his body. Her hands clutched at his back unconsciously, and she gasped when his mouth left hers to trail fire down her throat. Her head fell back to allow more room for his exploration, her heart hammering out of control.

The slight motion of the boat, which had been before just a sensation in the back of her consciousness, seemed to fill her now with a rhythm that surged and eased and throbbed, until her entire body seemed in motion. She was dizzy and breathless, and hollow with the need for him.

With a sudden impatient sound against the warmth of her throat, Rafferty lifted her into his arms and turned to stride toward their cabin. Sarah felt an instant's panic in that moment, a purely instinctive fear of the unknown, and pushed it aside fiercely. When he set her on her feet beside the turned-down bed her hands lifted to fumble inexpertly with the buttons of his shirt, and she concentrated on that task, and on the desire she felt, to keep the fear at bay.

Rafferty pushed the robe off her shoulders, his lips caressing her soft skin, and Sarah pulled her arms free of the lacy sleeves before struggling with his buttons again. She tugged the shirt from the waistband of his pants and slid her hands beneath the material, touching the smooth flesh covering his ribs. He seemed to tense even more at her touch, and his head lifted. Darkly flaming eyes gazed into hers, and the hard need in his face was softened into gentleness.

His hands caught hers and drew them to her sides, and his lips touched hers softly, again and again. "You're afraid," he murmured. "I don't want you to be afraid, my Sarah."

She realized only then that her hands were cold, that not even overwhelming desire could completely obliterate nervousness. She wanted to deny what was obvious, to reassure him of her own need, but no words could emerge past the tightness of her throat. She tried to tell him with her lips, responding eagerly to the touch of his, but the unknown was a watchful presence and they both sensed it.

Rafferty eased her back onto the bed, ignoring the trembling tension of his own body. One of his hands lay on her stomach, undemanding, and he stroked her hair back delicately with fingers that traced her face, her features, with a soft touch. His lips moved featherlight over her flushed skin, pressing her closed eyelids, grazing her cheeks, teasing her lips apart with gentle insistence.

Sarah was only vaguely aware that they lay in a pool of faint light spilling in from the other room, and she barely felt the softness of the bed beneath her. All her consciousness was focused on his lips, the nearness of his body, hard and warm. She couldn't breathe but didn't much care, and she was deeply grateful to the man she loved for the soothing caresses that were quieting her nebulous fears.

She tentatively lifted a hand when his lips reached the pulse pounding in her throat, touching his forearm and then his shoulder, understanding then that his care was costing him, because his muscles were tensed, rigid, and his skin was feverish. That more than anything partially laid her fears to rest, and her touch became firmer, stroking his shoulder and back compulsively, probing the taut, rippling muscles.

Rafferty murmured something low in his throat and gently guided her arms back to her sides, and she understood by his action that his control was strained unbearably by her touch. Obediently she lay still and restless, watching his face through desire-dazed eyes. Her fingers curled tightly into the sheets and she bit her lip to hold back the mindless sounds rising from some flaming core within her.

He was pressing kisses over her breastbone, and the lace straps of her nightgown were pushed slowly off her shoulders and down her arms. Then his hands slid up over her narrow ribcage until the swelling flesh of her breasts filled them, and she gasped at the intimate touch, losing what little breath she could still claim when his mouth found a pointed crest and closed on it hotly. The searing, wet caress shattered her senses and she moaned, the empty ache in her body growing and torturing her as his mouth teased.

Her breasts felt almost painful, abnormally sensitive, yet the hot suckling of his mouth and the rasp of his tongue was a pleasure beyond anything she'd ever known or imagined. She writhed with jerky, restless movements, unable to be still.

"Beautiful," he uttered thickly against her skin. His hands slid the nightgown down past her instinctively lifted hips, past her legs, and he tossed it aside. "You're so beautiful, my Sarah. So perfect." His rough palm swept down her side, curving over her hip and then sweeping back upward. His mouth remained on her breast, and he stroked her quivering belly in a gentle, circular motion.

"Rafferty . . ." She barely had the voice to speak at all, and his name was little more than a whisper. Her hands lifted again, desperate to touch him, and when he again refused to allow that she almost sobbed aloud with frustration. "I—I want to touch you."

"I know." His voice was raspy. "And I want you to. But not now. I can't—" He lifted his head, and the inferno within him flamed in his eyes. "Not just yet, darling. Close your eyes and let me love you."

Sarah obeyed, feeling an abrupt and almost savage wave of love for him sweep over her. She wanted to tell him, wanted to cry out her love, but her body's tension was growing and a sweet ache was building inexorably.

She could feel his hands on her thighs, caressing, guiding, and the hollowness swelled with his touch. She did cry out then as a surge of sheer pleasure lashed through her, heating her body as if her veins suddenly ran with fire. She was hardly conscious of his deep murmurs, all her senses concentrating on his intimate, incredibly pleasurable touch.

Her eyes snapped open, searching wildly for his face, focusing on it as he burned the already heated flesh of her breasts with his lips and stroked the throbbing, slick softness between her legs with a touch that was sure and heartstopping. Tension spiraled within her and she moaned again, her body moving of its own volition.

In some dim corner of her mind Sarah prepared to meet death, certain that it was impossible to feel this intensely and not die of the feeling. But there was no fear, not even fear of the unknown, and she could not have halted her body's instinctive, headlong rush toward release, no matter what.

She whispered his name over and over as ripples of pleasure grew ever stronger and stronger, until she had no voice left at all, until a sudden burst of sheer delight shattered the tension, and her body was gripped in waves of ecstasy that carried her somewhere she'd never been before and left her limp and trembling and stunned.

As she whispered his name, she became aware that he had left her side, and then she felt his hard, feverish body against her. He had, she realized, shed his clothing. In the faint light he was golden and powerful and beautiful, and a new infusion of strength and desire drove the weakness from her body. As badly as she had wanted him before, her desire now instantly climbed to new heights. Her ragged breathing matched his, and her body trembled as his warm, rough hands moved over it.

Fear, vanquished by the earlier passion he had evoked, didn't stir again even when he rose above her, and her body cradled him eagerly. She could touch him now, and did, her hands moving up his ribcage and over his chest, gripping his shoulders. He shuddered at her touch, his eyes closing briefly, and the strain of waiting made his face a taut mask. But even now, his every muscle rigid, Rafferty was gentle and careful.

He looked at her awakened face, and the utter trust in her eyes shook him badly, moved him unbearably. He was a moment away from shattering, all his instincts and senses raging in need. He wanted to bury himself in her, meld with her so completely that she would never be apart from him again. The slender softness of her body lay beneath him, inviting his possession with whispered pleas and a feverish heat, unknowingly chaining him to her with the unbreakable silken links of her trust.

He groaned harshly, scarcely aware of the sound, moving with exquisite care. He eased into her slowly, allowing her body to adjust to the alien touch, to accept him. Gazing into her widening eyes, he saw the flash of instinctive fear that was laced with wonder, and when the pain came he caught her soft cry in his mouth. He was still then, as her body struggled to accept him, and he waited until that inner tension gradually eased.

"Sarah?" His voice was hoarse, a thread of sound, and his body shuddered with the effort of control.

The hands gripping his shoulders slid up around

his neck and her wide eyes searched his face for an instant. Then she moved against him, impatience driving away all else.

Rafferty groaned again and began moving, and the fierce control over his body somehow heightened the sensations he felt. The hot velvet of her body sheathed his, holding him tightly, and her silky legs wrapped around his hips with a sensual, peculiarly feminine strength that drove him to the edge of madness. He couldn't get enough of her, couldn't ease the burning need blazing in his body. Far beyond physical passion and the need to possess was the wild, driving desire to become a part of her, to be absorbed by her until the very cells of her body were his.

She was a wild thing beneath him, her passionate response hot and demanding. Tension was building again, sweet and torturing, and her body arched upward, primitive with need. There was nothing left of the shy, cautious Sarah he had first met, and with that stripped away, she was all woman, abandoned and mindless with hunger.

She gave him all that she had to give, and Rafferty gave in return. There was no gentleness now. There was only fierce desire and a joining that transcended the physical.

Sarah wasn't aware of her own wild cries, and she was hardly conscious of the woman she had become. He was hers, *hers* and she gloried in that knowledge. Her powerful ripples of pleasure caught him within her in an explosive release. A harsh cry erupted from his throat, and he held her tightly to him as his own body found a shattering ecstasy.

Sarah absorbed the wonderful, heavy weight of him as he lay fully on her, her shaking arms holding him, and she was awed to realize she had never been whole until now. The sweetness of that realization moved her unbearably, and she was unaware of the tears that flowed from her eyes.

Rafferty lifted his head, easing his weight slightly, and his golden eyes darkened. A warm hand cupped her cheek and his thumb brushed the shining wetness from her temple.

"Because I hurt you?" he asked huskily.

She shook her head, turning her lips to kiss his palm. "No. Because I never knew. Because I love you."

He caught his breath, then kissed her gently. "I hope you mean that," he whispered. "Because I'll never let you go now."

She held him tightly, sweetly protesting when he moved. But her disappointment vanished when Rafferty lifted her into his arms and carried her from the room to the intimacy of a shared shower. She learned his body for the first time as warm water cascaded over it, and when at last he carried her back to their bed, exhaustion was forgotten.

Six

Sarah watched him sleep. There was, even in sleep, nothing innocent about him. The strength she had first sensed was plain now. His long, lean body was relaxed but there was a curious suggestion of tautness, an aura of latent power in the hard planes and angles.

She remembered her tiger-in-a-cage analogy, remembered once seeing just such a creature. Sleek, graceful even in stillness, the cat had exuded a raw, vital strength cloaked in beauty. And when vivid yellow eyes had opened, instantly alert, thousands of years of feline pride and power had gazed from their topaz depths.

She looked into Rafferty's eyes as they opened, and a surge of heat tingled throughout her body. The pride and the power were there, she saw, and with it a warm glow of love. Humbled, she wondered what generous fate had seen fit to gift her with this man's heart.

"I love you," she whispered.

He pulled her back down beside him, smiling tenderly. "I love you, my Sarah," he said, kissing her. "You're crying," he realized a moment later, concern tightening his features.

She managed a shaky laugh, and her fingers eased the tension from his face. "Because I love you. Because I feel so . . . lucky."

Rafferty smiled again. "Will you cry at our wedding?" he asked.

Sarah became still, gazing up at him. "Wedding?"

"Wedding. As in two people being joined in the bonds of matrimony."

She tried to think past the dizzying feeling of happiness. "It isn't very wise to make long-range plans in a situation like this," she reminded him in a husky voice.

He looked at her for a moment, still smiling. "Do you know how the dictionary defines *determined*, my Sarah?"

Silent, she waited.

"As 'fixed in purpose; resolute; firm.' That's me. I am quite determined that you will marry me."

"You're no shabby tiger," she whispered, almost to herself.

Clearly, Rafferty recognized the reference. His smile widened. "I'm glad you think so. And I assume that means you understand the definition of determined."

"Yes. I think I do." Her arms slid around his

neck. A few moments later, she said, "We didn't eat dinner."

"Who cares?"

They didn't eat breakfast either, at least not really. What they ate, somewhere around noon, was lunch. Harry, who cleared up last night's congealed meal, said not a word, and if anything he seemed more cheerful than usual while he served their lunch.

"I told you he was a romantic," Sarah observed when the cabin "boy" had gone. Then, in puzzlement, she added, "But how on earth did he know? The food?"

They were both fully dressed and eating with a deserved appetite, and Rafferty spared a moment to study her thoughtfully. Then he smiled. "There's just something about the morning after," he answered. "You're glowing."

Sarah resisted an urge to get up and look into a mirror. "Am I? Well," she said firmly, "you look different too."

"I didn't notice it when I shaved."

"You'll notice it when male lawyers stop underestimating you in court."

Rafferty looked startled. "Assuming you're right about that, why would they stop? I have exactly the same face I had last night, and for a considerable number of years before."

Sarah half saluted him with her coffee cup, smiling. "It's not the face, it's what's under it.

Nobody is every again going to think you're a tamed tiger."

He reached across the small table to cover her hand with his, having discovered that touching her was as necessary to him now as breathing. "Is that supposed to make sense?" he wondered.

"It makes sense. To me, and to you." Her smile widened. "Your two friends know it as well. They were both very wary of you on the island. Explosions in the past?"

Rafferty wasn't surprised by her perception for he had realized she was a strongly intuitive woman. "One or two. In addition to being friends, we've worked together several times on projects related to our boss's highly visible business affairs."

"For instance?" She was definitely curious.

He reflected for a moment. "A few years ago, there was a kidnapping threat. Josh was in the middle of some tricky negotiations and refused to accept protection. Zach was with him twenty-four hours a day, of course, and he's more of a bodyguard than most men ever need. Lucas was running down every lead we could dig up, and I was involved in the legal aspect of the business negotiations. Then, right out from under all our noses, Josh vanished."

"What happened?" she asked, intrigued.

"Well, we were all under standing orders not to go public if something like that happened. We alerted Josh's stepfather and sister and Zach sent some of the security team out to keep an eye on them. I stalled the business negotiations without letting them know anything was wrong."

Rafferty brooded for a moment in silence, obviously thinking about that occasion, and Sarah could see that he was still bothered by the memory. She waited patiently, and after a time he went on.

"Relatively speaking, I was the new kid on the team; Zach's been with Josh nearly fifteen years, and Lucas almost ten. I'd been with him just over a year, and it had taken that long for me to become familiar with both his business affairs and his personality. I knew Zach and Lucas, of course, but not well, and they hardly knew me. What I *did* know, however, was that Zach's security was airtight, that Josh was as close to him as a brother, and that Josh had a rather unsettling habit of doing dangerous things instead of paying other people to do them for him."

"He hadn't been kidnapped," she guessed.

"Bingo," Rafferty said with a sigh. "They hadn't expected me to see it, because I *was* new on the team. But before I had accepted Josh's offer to be his attorney, I'd checked him out, and I knew quite a bit of his background. So I knew he hated to just sit and wait, letting someone else control his life. But when he vanished, naturally my first thought was that someone had gotten to him."

"But he vanished on his own."

"Exactly. He told Zach to put everything on hold, then more or less picked up his car keys and disappeared. Went underground."

Sarah couldn't help but smile. "I always thought that sounded so romantic—going underground."

Rafferty grinned a little. "It isn't. And you wouldn't think someone with Josh's fairly famous profile could get away with it. But somehow he does. Since he's no dummy, he realized that the kidnapping threat was tied in with the negotiations. *Somebody* didn't want him to take over that company. He went underground to find out who—with a minimum of fuss and bother. He got in touch with his intelligence contacts, and they went to work."

"But you didn't know that."

"I didn't know that. And, having a suspicious mind, I couldn't help wondering if maybe Zach or Lucas—the only two besides myself to know the complete security setup—might possibly have turned traitor."

"Ouch," she said.

"Uh-huh. I'd seen too many cases of an insider going bad, so I could hardly rule it out. I was hamstrung by Josh's orders and I didn't dare trust anyone else. And there was a hell of a lot more at stake besides the life of a man I'd grown to like and respect very much; his disappearance or, heaven forbid, death would send stock markets all over the world into tailspins. Josh Long *is* his company, and thousands depend on him for employment."

"And you couldn't just sit and wait."

"No. I knew there was a possibility he'd vanished on his own, but I couldn't be sure. So I did some checking. It took several days, and in the meantime I was stonewalling the negotiations with every excuse I could think up. Zach and Lucas were going through the motions of looking for him, but it didn't ring true. Then, about the time I'd decided to confront the two of them and get a straight answer, one of the partners in this company we'd been negotiating with suddenly started a rumor that Josh had been kidnapped."

"He got nervous," Sarah decided.

"Definitely nervous. We found out later that the men he'd hired to do the job had disappeared—Josh's intelligence contacts had found them pretty quickly—and since he couldn't get in touch with them he had no way of knowing if they actually had Josh. On the other hand, the men had been hired through middlemen, so they didn't know who had ordered the kidnapping. Stalemate. *If* I had known what Josh was up to, I'd have been in the perfect position to sit and wait for somebody to start squirming. As it was, all I had to go on were my own suspicions and a paper trail that told me this particular partner had the most to lose by the takeover."

"What did you do?"

Rafferty grinned. "I busted it wide open."

"How?"

"Well, suspicion aside, I didn't really believe that Zach or Lucas had kidnapped Josh. At the same time, I was mad as hell over the entire situation. I don't like being caught in a poker game with blank cards."

Sarah gazed at him, seeing again the tiger who assumed protective coloration. "I see. And so?"

"Orders or no, I wasn't about to sit and do nothing. So I gathered the paper evidence, contacted a friend of *mine* in the intelligence community, and spilled the beans. That gave the authorities both ends of the trail, and the nervous partner was quietly hauled away in the middle of his lunch. An hour later, Josh came home."

"What'd he say?"

Rafferty grimaced and rubbed the back of his neck. "I'm afraid I didn't give him much of a chance to say anything. First I tendered my resignation, and then I really flew off the handle. He couldn't get a word in for ten minutes, and Zach and Lucas just stood there with their mouths open. I must have surprised them," he finished reflectively.

"Must have," she agreed. She cleared her throat. "You still work for him."

"Yes, well. I'm not exactly sure how that came about. Josh talked a lot. Zach and Lucas talked a lot. And then we all four got drunk. When I stumbled into the office the next morning, my resignation was on my desk, torn neatly in half. I felt too lousy to protest."

Sarah couldn't help but laugh. "I'd like to see you drunk. Hagen says you can tell a man's true nature when he's had a few too many."

"That just might be true. Josh gets very gallant and very humorous after a few. Zach smiles a lot and makes everybody nervous. Lucas would storm hell with a glass of water."

"And Rafferty?"

"Rafferty just gets silly."

"Next time we run into your friends, I'm going to ask them."

"But I told you."

"Ummm. I've a feeling they'd tell me something different."

He smiled a little. "Maybe. How about you?"

"Drunk?" Sarah looked innocent. "Rafferty, I don't get drunk."

He eyed her suspiciously. "Uh-huh."

"Darling, I never have—"

Sarah didn't get a chance to further defend her claim, mainly because Rafferty more or less attacked her. She didn't realize why until a considerable time later when they were lying together on the bed in a tangle of arms and legs and clothing and exhaustion.

In a bemused voice, she asked, "Are you going to do that every time I call you darling?"

Rafferty's change from a state of prostration to one of revitalization took roughly five seconds.

"It triggers your libido?" she managed faintly sometime later.

"It triggers something."

Siran kept his eyes on the couple at the bow while he put through a call on the radio. "It won't work," he reported tersely. "A blind man wouldn't believe a fight between them. Over."

"That's impossible," the voice returned flatly. "Every eventuality has been covered. Over."

"Then you missed something." Siran's voice changed, and as if he were speaking to an equal, he said, "They're in love, and love on the edge of a knife is unpredictable. In any case, it's my judgment that no observer would find an argument between them believable. Over."

Words sprinkled with brimstone came from the voice not known to use them. "All right. I'll devise another plan. Unless you hear from me before, cross the three-mile limit late tomorrow morning. Understood? Over."

"Understood. Over and out." Siran replaced the microphone and shook his head a little as he watched the couple. The threshold of hell, he thought, was a damned unsteady place to conduct a love affair. He could only hope theirs would bond them together, make a team of them. He had seen it happen.

Once or twice.

Joshua Long held the microphone and gazed at his wife of several weeks, both of them listening intently to the voice droning steadily on. When there was a break in the officious voice, Josh pressed the call button and spoke firmly.

"Stop explaining; it wouldn't make sense to anyone except you and Machiavelli. Let's hear some suggestions for straightening out the mess."

Five minutes later, Josh signed off and gave his wife an eloquent look.

"I know," Raven said meekly. "It's my fault you got involved with him in the first place."

Josh pulled her close and kissed her. "I don't regret you," he explained quite unnecessarily. "Just him. Anyone in his right mind would regret Hagen. And I'd like to know how in hell he found out the *Corsair* was here in the Caribbean."

"I don't think we really want to know that," Raven said. "It would probably give us both a Big Brother complex. Anyway, if he's telling us all of the truth—and heaven only knows if he is—then this plan he's concocted seems sound. At least as far as it goes." She frowned and rubbed her cheek against this chest. "An awful lot seems to be riding on Sereno's reactions."

Obviously enjoying the feeling of his wife's soft curves pressed against him, Josh said absently, "Too much. Unless, that is, a piece of the puzzle is still missing. Want to bet Hagen's kept just one *tiny* item of information to himself?"

"Not really, no."

"I don't blame you." He frowned a little. "I just might be about to make a formidable enemy."

Disturbed, Raven tipped her head back to search his face. "Sereno certainly won't be happy with you if he connects Rafferty and Sarah to the disappearance of the information, especially if those terrorists discover he welcomed them onto the island. You'll owe him after this. In a big way."

"Yes. Oddly enough, I think he'll be fair in collecting the debt. He didn't strike me as a man to let temper get the better of him."

"Darling, I know you want to help Rafferty, but he wouldn't thank you if you had to compromise your principles or make a bad enemy to do it. You won't, will you?"

Josh laughed. "No, I won't. I've kept an eye on Kadeira since I met Sereno, and I think there's a method to the man's ruthlessness. I don't condone his method, but the goal is one I agree with. Besides, even though I'm gambling that he'll play fair, it isn't that big a risk. He's too proud to ask for much in return for a favor. Even a favor that costs him personally."

"How much is much?"

Josh dropped a kiss on the top of her head. "Well, he won't ask me to arm his fleet." Then he turned back toward the radio.

Almost to herself, Raven muttered, "His fleet's already armed."

Josh sent her a rueful glance of agreement, but concentrated on putting through a call to the island of Kadeira. He spoke in flawless Spanish, identifying himself and asking for President Sereno.

He got him.

Sarah sat up determinedly and looked down at the man stretched out lazily beside her in the double lounge. "We're not acting at all like agents on the day before a serious mission," she told him severely.

One golden eye opened and then closed again. "No, I suppose not," Rafferty agreed. "Should we put on our trench coats?"

"Very funny."

He sighed. "I'm trying not to think about tomorrow," he explained, opening both eyes to stare up at her wryly. "For several reasons, not the least of which is that I don't want to have to fake a fight and yell at you."

"Well, I don't want to yell at you, either."

"That will not be necessary."

Both jumped in surprise and turned their heads to find that Siran had approached cat-footed. His face was expressionless.

"Word has come from Hagen," he told them. "It is no longer required that you fake a disagreement. President Sereno will welcome you on the island."

"Why?" Rafferty asked bluntly.

"I have no idea, Mr. Lewis." And his tone said that he didn't particularly care whether Rafferty believed that. "We will cross the three-mile limit tomorrow just before noon. We will be met and escorted to port. You will be invited to stay in the presidential residence." He turned and retreated.

Sarah looked at Rafferty. "How do you like that?"

"I don't." He was frowning. "Look, are you *sure* that Sereno was in love with a woman who looked just like you?"

"Positive," she said immediately. "There were some news clippings—foreign correspondents, of course, since there's no longer a free press in Kadeira. I looked up the stuff myself. The reporters were gleeful that an American girl he met in Trinidad could have such a powerful effect on Sereno. Somebody managed to get a picture of them together. Looking at that Sara was like looking in a mirror."

"All right. But the original plan was for us to stage a fight, presumably within Sereno's sight.

Your resemblance to his love was supposed to do the trick after that."

"Yes. And so?"

"If I understood Siran correctly, we're now *expected* on Kadeira."

"It did sound like that," she said slowly.

"Then I don't get it. Why would we be expected—and welcomed—in advance? Who told him we were coming?"

It was Sarah who realized the truth, partly because she knew from other agents how Hagen worked, and partly because of her own natural ability to see logical patterns in things.

"Rafferty, does Josh Long trade in favors?"

"He's been known to. Business is like that." Rafferty stared at her and sat up slowly. "No. Not even *Hagen* would . . ."

"Think about it," she urged. "Hagen's got us invading the island on the flimsiest of pretexts. Then he finds out—and you know he *would*—that Josh Long is nearby. Nearby, and with at least one past meeting with Sereno to his credit. Now he knows there isn't a businessman in the world, island dictator or not, who wouldn't be delighted to do your boss a favor. Especially a simple favor. Like welcoming a honeymoon couple into an island paradise with a little bit of once-in-a-lifetime pomp and ceremony."

Rafferty said something violent.

Sarah looked at him with sympathy. "From all I've heard, Hagen's got the gall to ask that. Question is, would Josh go along with it?"

Rafferty looked a bit calmer, but none too happy.

"Yes. For the possibility of stopping a terrorist organization. And to save my hide and yours."

"He doesn't know me."

"You're one of Hagen's beautiful but misguided victims. He has a soft spot for those. And Zach and Lucas have probably told him by now that I'm in love with you. That'd be enough for Josh. But, dammit, it puts him in a hell of a position. From men like Sereno, favors don't come cheap."

Sarah waited silently. That unexpected strength was evident in Rafferty's handsome face, and she knew that he had to come to terms with this himself. Because he knew Josh. Because he knew what this would cost Josh. She didn't remind him that they could still pull out. They both knew that option was open at least until tomorrow.

After a moment, he said quietly, "I could rationalize. Josh is a hardheaded businessman with nearly twenty years of experience in handling people who want something from him. He hates terrorists with a vengeance. And only once have I seen him wade into a situation where he wasn't in control." Golden eyes focused on her, and Rafferty reached out to cup her cheek warmly. "When he fell in love."

She waited.

"If you're right about this—and I think you are—then I have to believe Josh knows what he's doing. But I'll owe him."

"We'll owe him."

He pulled her down beside him on the lounge, closing his arms around her tightly.

• • •

They went below deck for dinner that evening, but returned to their lounge on the deck afterwards. The boat was making little headway, since they were already close to Kadeira and were more or less circling the island leisurely. It was cool on deck, and quiet, except for the low hum of the engine and the rhythmic splashing of water against the hull. Tom, Dick, and Harry were playing cards in their quarters, and Siran, as always, was on the bridge, alone and watchful.

Rafferty could hardly help but think of Siran's soundless feet, especially when Sarah responded to his kisses with whispered endearments and that surprising fire of hers. Biting back a groan, he muttered, "I'd like to hang a bell round Siran's neck."

Sarah had no difficulty in following the statement back to its source. Feathering her lips along his jaw, she said, "He does tend to interrupt, doesn't he?"

"Yes, damn him."

'Umm." She moved suddenly and slid off the lounge. "Wait here, all right?"

"What're you—" But she was gone, vanishing into the darkness. Rafferty lay on his back and stared up at the stars, wondering what she was up to. He didn't have to wait long to find out; she was back in moments. Her slight weight settled on the edge of the lounge, and fingers that had rapidly become expert at the task coped with the buttons of his shirt.

Rafferty could almost hear his heart go into double-time. "Sarah?"

In the soft, honeyed voice that was itself a caress, she murmured, "They were all very polite and agreeable. Nobody's coming up on deck, and Captain Siran plans to remain on the bridge indefinitely—where he can't see us."

"You asked them—?" Rafferty thought of the Sarah he'd first met, cautious, unawakened, and shy, and a heady delight raced through him at this evidence of abandon.

"Why shouldn't I ask them?" She allowed him to sit up just long enough to shrug off his shirt, then pressed him back down onto the lounge. Her hands moved over his chest, and she bent to press her lips warmly in the dark gold mat of hair. "I wanted to make love to you."

He caught his breath as small fires blazed to life beneath her touch, spreading and meeting one another until he was burning all over, burning and throbbing. "I'd—be crazy to say no," he managed hoarsely.

She was little more than a shadow in darkness, curiously insubstantial with her black caftan blending into the night, and her hair a dark glow as she bent over him. But she was real, real and loving, and her loving desire more than made up for a lack of experience. With aching tenderness, she caressed his flesh, tracing shoulders and chest and ribs. Her soft lips found his flat nipples and teased them hard, then followed the arrow-shaped trail of hair to his belt buckle.

Her delicate hands unfastened his belt and pants, and Rafferty never knew if he helped her to discard the clothing or if she managed the feat alone. He had known from the first that her touch brought a sweet madness, and the test of his willpower on that first night was nothing compared to the effort it took now for him to remain still beneath her hands. But he fought the primitive urges to assume control, knowing they would both find a special pleasure in this.

And it was in awed delight that Sarah felt his building response, felt him quiver beneath her touch. What had begun in a spurt of reckless desire had become something wondrous and almost painfully exquisite. The faintly salty taste of his skin, the rough brush of hair, the sleekness of hard muscles, all made her dizzy and hungry. She could feel the soft breeze and hear the rushing and splashing of the ocean, but nothing was real to her except him. Nothing existed but them.

She trailed her soft hands slowly down his sides, shaping strong hips and thighs, teasing him partly by instinct and partly with a newfound knowledge. Her lips were warm, exploring his body as he had explored hers. There was no shyness now, no reluctance or hesitation, and his taut readiness fueled her hunger with every passing second.

His fingers curled into the cushions beneath him and Rafferty groaned aloud, his muscles rigid with the effort of enduring her shattering caresses. Every rasping breath burned his chest achingly, and his heart was choking him with its pounding. The pleasure was so intense it was as if she had scalded away his flesh and now tormented raw nerves.

His control splintered with a suddenness that

was almost audible, and she was moving even as he did, both reaching for the snaps that fastened her caftan. The material flew out to either side of her, hanging from her shoulders and leaving her bare body glowing against a backdrop of sheer black, and she hardly needed his guiding hands on her hips as he pulled her over him. And the sound he made when he thrust into the welcoming heat of her was a primitive growl of satisfaction.

They were both still for a heartbeat, fused, one, breath suspended and bodies quivering on the edge of a tormenting precipice. In that eternal moment, Rafferty thought that he had never seen so clearly, so starkly. She was a pure white flame in the darkness, slender, steely, burning, delicate, incredibly feminine, impossibly strong. And he belonged to her heart and soul.

Then the stillness splintered, and they were moving, driven by identical needs, rushing into a bottomless chasm and to a willing death. Locked together.

Her slight weight was a caress, and Rafferty held her with his remaining strength, vaguely aware that her caftan had floated about them both in a silky covering. He could feel the breeze cooling heated flesh, feel her lips moving against his throat, and there were no words for what his heart felt. Except the most simple ones.

"I love you."

She raised herself just a bit. "I love you too," she said solemnly, still just a little breathless. "And how on earth did we wind up making love on the deck of a yacht?"

"I was attacked and undressed by a shameless wanton," he explained. "I don't know about you."

"I don't know about me, either. I just seemed to go crazy all of a sudden." She buried her face against his throat again, and he felt as well as heard a giggle escape. "I can't *believe* I really looked those men in the eye and told them not to disturb us."

"I wish I'd been a fly on the wall," he said wistfully.

"Ummm." She lifted her head again and kissed him. In a tone of pleased discovery, she added, "And I didn't even have to call you darling."

He cleared his throat. "Sarah?"

She could feel the stirring of his body, a renewal of desire. "This is incredible," she said, bemused. "What if I say it in public?"

"We'll find a closet," he murmured, threading his fingers through her hair and feeling more than a little bemused himself.

"There must be magic in the word," she decided. But she rapidly lost interest in the analytical aspect of the matter.

It wasn't important.

It was late when they managed to find the strength to make their way down to the cabin. They showered together, luxuriating in the privacy and intimacy, then lay together, pleasantly exhausted, in bed. But both were conscious that tomorrow was really the beginning of their dangerous assignment, and neither could sleep.

"If something happens—" she began.

Rafferty pulled her even closer, one hand stroking her silky hair. "Nothing will happen."

Softly, she said, "We can't ignore reality."

"No," he agreed, but his tone was fierce. "We can't. But we have an appointment at the altar when this is finished, and nothing is going to prevent that."

Sarah rubbed her cheek against his chest, smiling, feeling a sense of certainty about the future for the first time. "Determined," she said lazily. He was determined, and who could stand in his way?

Seven

President Sereno commanded an impressive fleet. As the *Thespian* crossed the three-mile limit late the following morning, those aboard the yacht waited in varying states of unease to be noticed. Within ten minutes two fast boats resembling coast guard cutters swept around them and then came alongside. Both vessels were openly armed and the uniformed men aboard them carried automatic weapons.

The crew of the *Thespian* was directed in crisp English via a loudspeaker to maintain their heading and speed and, needless to say, they obeyed the order.

As the island of Kadeira became more visible on the horizon, it was Rafferty who noticed several of their escorts staring at Sarah in surprise. It was likely that her bright hair and the slender figure she presented dressed in white slacks and a green blouse had first drawn their eyes, but even with the distance between the boats it was clear they thought they recognized her.

"I guess Sereno didn't keep his feeling to himself, even around his men," Rafferty observed to Sarah as they stood on deck together. "The men look like they've seen a ghost."

Sarah barely noticed. She was scanning the horizon off to starboard where a large group of vessels maneuvered in some mysterious pattern in the distance, reminding herself silently that she had known they were sailing into an armed fortress. Still, the size of those distant ships was unsettling. She looked up at Rafferty, and his faint smile soothed her nerves while his steady golden gaze gave her courage.

She leaned against his side, then felt a new uneasiness raise its head: Rafferty's gun was packed in his suitcase, ready to be carried onto the island. "If someone searches our bags and finds the gun . . ." she murmured.

He shook his head a little. "I doubt it would raise suspicions. We're supposed to be wealthy, remember? I wouldn't be the first rich man to carry a gun."

They turned their attention forward, watching as the boats entered the harbor of the crescent-shaped island. It was a good harbor with plenty of room for the score of vessels riding at anchor and tied up the dock. Except for a few fishing boats, all belonged to the military.

A cluster of buildings, mostly the warehouses common in such areas, stood near the dock. To the left was the striking vista of towering mountains and rolling hills that helped to make the island so beautiful, and to the right, whitewashed and shining in the bright sunlight, was the island's only real city and the home of most of its people.

No building reached more than five stories, and all the whitewash couldn't hide the scarring evidence of a country in turmoil. There was some construction going on, but not much, and shored-up buildings showed like broken teeth in the skyline. Colorful flowers struggled gallantly in the rubble of the bombed remains of cars, trucks, and buildings.

As they slowed and prepared to dock, they could see armed men in uniform all around, guarding the buildings and walking the streets in pairs. None of them even reacted to the distant stutter of weapons off in the hills, nor was there a reaction from the colorfully dressed people who went expressionlessly about the business of living.

Sarah felt a lump in her throat, and was hardly conscious of engines dying and the thumps of the yacht settling against the dock. Kadeira could have been a beautiful island, she thought; it *was* a beautiful island—being choked to death.

Tourism and foreign investment might save it even at this late date, but few visitors or investors would have been willing to put their lives or their money at stake in a country where battles took place daily and "rebels" from the hills periodically attacked the city.

The government that Sereno had overthrown

years before had been a brutal one, a leech sucking the life out of the island's people. A young and handsome general then in the revolutionary army, Sereno had practically been carried into power on the shoulders of his men after having become a legend of the uprising.

For a time, there had been peace. Sereno had set about the inevitably slow and understandably complicated task of patching and rebuilding a country in tatters, a country of aching poverty, a shattered economy, and a populace weary of both. He had promised a better life, and had, by all accounts, tried his best to deliver on that promise.

It wasn't entirely clear to anyone what had happened then. Perhaps it had been impatience on the part of some at the slowness of change, or a power struggle within his government. Whatever the reason, revolution had broken out again. A general who had been Sereno's comrade in the early days became a bitter enemy, taking to the hills from which he periodically stormed the city, and Kadeira was once again plunged into civil war.

"It's a shame, isn't it?" Rafferty asked quietly, and Sarah forced herself to put speculation out of her mind.

"Yes. A shame."

Their attention was attracted by bustle on the dock then, and they watched as a gleaming black limousine flying the flags of state drew to a stop. There were Jeeps in front of and behind the limo, and when the vehicles halted, soldiers got out and stood with guns at the ready. The limo's passenger didn't wait for the door to be opened for him, but thrust it wide and got out.

"That isn't Sereno," Sarah observed as Rafferty helped her onto the dock.

"I'm not surprised," Rafferty responded quietly, as they stood together and watched the approach of a slender man of medium height. He possessed a military carriage, despite the absence of a uniform. "Sereno's a target no guards could protect effectively out in the open like this."

Sarah could feel no tension in Rafferty, and she was amazed even though she knew he wasn't a man to get nervous—until she realized that she herself was relaxed and curiously detached. The wondering was over, and the time for doubts past. They were in this now, and the only way out was to finish what they'd been sent here to do. The realization was comforting.

The man reached them, his last steps faltering when his cool gaze fell on Sarah. His surprise was obvious, as was his dismay, but both emotions were quickly hidden. His voice was clipped when he spoke, his English perfect. "I am Colonel Durant, aide to President Sereno."

"Rafferty Lewis. My wife, Sarah."

How easily he says that! she thought, feeling happy as she inclined her head politely in response to Durant's brief bow.

Abruptly, the colonel asked, "Have we met, Mrs. Lewis?"

"No, Colonel, we haven't," she responded calmly. She met his hard stare, and knew the exact moment when Durant realized she merely resembled, but was not, the Sara he had known.

"Welcome to Kadeira," Durant told them. "President Sereno extends his compliments and invites you to stay at his home while you are here. He asked me to assure you that your yacht will be protected, and the comfort of your crew seen to."

Rafferty glanced over his shoulder and saw Siran's dark face remain expressionless at the assurance. He looked back at Durant. "Thank you, Colonel."

"My men will see to your luggage." He made a slight gesture and two men detached themselves from the rest and headed for the *Thespian*. Then Durant gestured toward his car, leading the way.

As the limousine wound through the city streets, the scars of Kadeira were even more visible. There were bombed buildings and shops with shuttered windows. Rotting vegetables were thrown at the gleaming car from the obscurity of alleyways. But there were a few construction crews at work, their efforts guarded by soldiers and Jeeps with machine guns mounted in them, and a handful of shops were open for business.

They passed a radio station, its windows and doors boarded up and the tower behind it a shorn-off mass of twisted metal. And they passed the prison.

Though he had commented on nothing else, Durant did direct their attention to the low, square building with barred windows and an impressive number of guards patrolling it. Martial law was, of course, in effect, he explained, but the streets were safe; the rebels had been driven into the hills after their last foray into town some days before.

He made no comment on the vegetables thrown, though it was clear evidence of the disillusionment felt by the city's people for their government.

Less than half a mile from the prison was the presidential home and if Rafferty and Sarah had expected a palatial estate, they were disappointed. Both saw a huge and imposing building looming on their left, but instead of stopping there the car turned in the opposite direction. Either seeing or sensing their surprise, Durant explained that the building they had just passed was the old presidential palace, turned into a hospital when Sereno came to power.

Rafferty and Sarah made no comment, but they glanced at each other, and both of them read the identical thought: There was, it seemed, some decency in Sereno's regime. Shades of gray.

Both were also aware that Durant had quite deliberately drawn their attention to the prison, and they could only believe it had been a subtle warning of what happened to enemies of the state. For Sarah especially, it was sobering.

After passing through a guarded gate, the limousine stopped in the curving driveway in front of a two-storied building finished in stucco. As the residence of one man, it was somewhat imposing, but there was nothing palatial about the house.

Multicolored flowers typical of the island had been planted in beds and boxes around the outside in an effort soften the stark whiteness of the building, and some attempt had been made to fashion the window bars in a decorative style meant to partially soften the impact of their bleak purpose.

As they got out of the car, Rafferty saw guards strategically but unobtrusively placed all around the house, and he knew that Sarah had seen them as well. Both of them heard the hollow clanging of a cell door closing behind them, and they followed Durant into the house.

They were shown into a book-lined room, too informal to be an office, and were politely asked to wait while Durant went to inform their host of their arrival. Rafferty, seeing the expression on Sarah's face, asked, "What?"

She looked at him. "Oh, it's just that I *like* this house, and I didn't expect to." Glancing toward the closed door, she reached into her purse and drew out what looked like a small transistor radio; it could be used as a normal radio, but when buttons were pushed in a certain sequence, it became instead a device for detecting tiny microphones.

After a moment, she replaced the radio in her purse. "Clear. How paranoid *is* paranoid?"

"You mean us?" Rafferty smiled a little. "In this situation, we shouldn't ask that question too often. Best not to take chances." He looked around the room, interested. "But I know what you mean about the house. It's nice, but very simple and comfortable."

"Hardly the home of a megalomaniac." She lifted an eyebrow at him quizzically. "Shades of gray?"

Rafferty moved uneasily to a set of French doors which opened onto a terrace. "I wish I knew. I've a feeling we'll have to throw out everything we've heard about the man and trust our instincts. I also have a feeling," he turned to stare at her, "that this assignment isn't nearly as simple as I thought—and was told. There's more at stake here, isn't there? Not merely a transfer of information."

Sarah perched on the arm of a flowered sofa and sighed. She met his steady gaze, her own faintly pleading. "Hagen can be very persuasive."

Rafferty didn't look hurt or offended, merely resigned. "I thought so. He talked a lot to you about one's word being one's bond, and then got you to promise to keep something to yourself awhile?"

"I hate being manipulated," she said somewhat fiercely. "I think he brainwashed me."

"Well, I don't blame you for keeping your word, however he managed to extract it from you. When were you supposed to tell me the rest?"

"Once we got here."

"Past the point of no return? It figures."

She glanced toward the closed door and lowered her voice. "We *are* here for information, but it isn't written down. It's in someone's head. You, uh, recall the toy manufacturer from Billings?"

Rafferty sighed. "Don't tell me."

"Yes. It seems Sereno wasn't so paranoid after all, I guess. The man was working undercover, and was gathering information on the terrorist organization. We—we have to get him out of prison and off the island."

He stared at her, somewhat dazed. "We have to—? Sarah, my love, my darling, are you out of your mind? Did you *see* that prison?"

Despite everything, Sarah almost wanted to laugh at his despairing horror. But she didn't. She cleared her throat. "Yes. Depressing, wasn't it?"

"So Hagen never intended for you to use your skills as a cryptographer, right?"

She nodded.

"And he chose you because of your resemblance to the other Sarah?"

Again she nodded. "What did Hagen do, demand your firstborn child as forfeit if you didn't agree to this insanity?"

Sarah lifted her hands in a helpless gesture and looked bewildered. "I know it's irrational. I knew it when he briefed me, dammit. And I don't know why I agreed. I really don't! It just seemed to happen somehow."

Rafferty went to her and lifted one hand to his lips. Very gently, he said, "After this, I'm going to keep you away from salesmen, politicians, and other unscrupulously charming people. They seem to have an odd effect on you. I am also going to kill Hagen at the first opportunity."

Sarah conjured up a rueful smile. "I've been meaning to tell you that I—I tend to buy things I don't really need if people ask me to."

Rafferty asked the ceiling for inspiration and clearly got no reply. He looked back at Sarah. "At least tell me Hagen knew the layout of the prison?

And put together something remotely resembling a plan so we can do this insane thing?"

"Of course he had a plan."

"Well?"

Sarah didn't know whether to be relieved or annoyed when the opening door kept her from replying. She got to her feet. Still holding Rafferty's hand, but a bit more tightly now, and both turned to meet their host.

Photographs and television tend to flatten a personality and rob it of much of its life and sparkle, and so a truly charming and charismatic person first met through the media often seems overwhelming when met in the flesh. That was quite definitely the case with President Sereno.

He was unusual among his countrymen, in that he was over six feet tall and powerfully built. He was dressed casually in a white shirt unbuttoned at the throat, and dark slacks. But the informal attire did nothing to conceal the physical strength of broad shoulders and powerful limbs or the honed grace of his movements. He was dark, black-haired and black-eyed, his lean face handsome and bearing none of the marks of his reportedly difficult and violent life.

But there had to be scars, Sarah thought, inside if not outside. It was evident that Sereno didn't wear his where they could be seen. He could have been taken for a man ten years younger than his thirty-eight years.

"Good afternoon. I'm Andrés Sereno." His English was easy and idiomatic, the accent faintly American due to the American mercenary who had taught him to speak the language when he was little more than a child. His voice was deep and calm and sure, a voice that could move a country.

Sarah watched as he came forward to shake Rafferty's hand, and she barely heard the introduction. She saw that Sereno's shoulders were braced, as if to ward off a blow. And she felt, with a woman's intuitive awareness, that although he had been prepared by his colonel to see her, Durant had not entirely convinced him she was not his Sara.

She offered her hand by instinct, and realized when she felt the faint chill of his that he was nervous. Then she met his black eyes, and saw a very small light go out in them.

She agreed with none of his policies and had come prepared to despise him. She had been shocked by his wounded country. She felt no attraction to him as a man although she was aware of his sheer magnetism. She was appalled by his willingness to shelter terrorists in his country, even if he didn't aid them with arms or influence. And she was quite definitely afraid of the danger he posed to Rafferty and herself.

But in that flashing instant, when she looked up at him, what she saw in his eyes almost broke her heart.

Nearly an hour later, after having been shown through the lovely garden and house by their charming host, been given drinks, and shared casual conversation, they found themselves in a light, airy suite on the second floor. Their luggage had been unpacked. They found Rafferty's gun lying innocently in the drawer of the nightstand, still loaded. And Sarah had automatically checked and found the rooms clear of listening devices or other troublesome electronics.

"You're not in danger of succumbing to him, are you?" Rafferty asked her, but it was clear from his tone that he knew it wasn't true and also knew she was troubled.

Sarah sat on the wide bed and lifted her shoulders in a shrug, puzzled. "No, no. I just can't figure him out. We *know* the things he's done, he doesn't deny them himself, and yet . . . There's this house, and the hospital, and his welcome of us—and *him*, dammit."

"All of which," Rafferty pointed out quietly, "can be explained with the rest. What better way to endear himself to his people than by living simply and turning the former presidential palace into a hospital to help them, assuming he managed to supply and staff the hospital? As for his welcome—he's doing a favor for a powerful man, and fully expects one in return. And we knew he was charismatic before we got here."

"I know. It makes sense."

"But you aren't convinced?"

"He left your gun."

"I'll admit that has me a bit bothered. I'm sure the servants reported it to him, though. And, as I said, I wouldn't be the first wealthy man to carry one for protection, especially in a place like this."

"And he doesn't mind your having it in his own house? With assassination plots springing up around here daily—almost hourly?"

"Maybe Josh told him I feel safer with a gun but that I'm not really into shooting island presidents."

Sarah gestured. "All right, all right. At least now we know for sure that Josh did call him; he didn't hesitate to tell us that, did he?"

"No." Rafferty went over to the window and looked out. The house was built on a slight rise so that the town lay spread out below. "Nor did he hesitate to give us full run of the city—unescorted, if we prefer. I think we'll take his advice, though, and not venture anywhere else. Judging by the gunfire we heard, the hills sound a bit dangerous for visitors. And those terrorists are around here somewhere."

"He didn't mention them."

"No. And I doubt the group would want to dirty up their backyard by attacking guests of the president. Things like that tend to wear out your welcome. Still, you never know. Better not to take chances."

Sarah smiled at him when he turned to face her. "You're being very calm and professional about all these surprises, I must say. It's very comforting."

"I believe it's called being shell-shocked. I don't think anything could surprise me now. So I suppose I should hear about this grand plan of Hagen's."

"Sure you want to take the plunge?"

"I'm braced and ready."

"All right." Sarah banked pillows behind her

back and leaned against the headboard. "First of all, I can't be sure just *when* we have to move. Hagen said we would receive a, quote, unmistakable signal, end quote. Probably within a few days, a week at the most."

"He'll probably send up a rocket or something," Rafferty said in a wry tone.

Sarah was surprised. "You sound as if he's watching us as we speak."

Rafferty gave her a confident look. "Trust me. If your boss isn't actually on this island, then he's probably out in the Caribbean in a submarine or on a battleship. Gleefully rubbing his pudgy little hands together while he watches—through an infrared camera or something—the strands of his insidious, sticky web being woven into place."

Sarah looked doubtful, but continued. "When we receive the signal, we prepare to move. At *exactly* noon, we're to be at the prison. I've seen a diagram of the place, and I'll sketch it for you beforehand."

"That memory of yours is coming in handy."

"It saves time and trouble," she admitted dryly. "There's a back door to which I have a key, and I have a key to the cell—"

"I haven't seen them," Rafferty observed.

"They're in one of my shoes."

"In a hollow heel?" he asked, hopeful.

"As a matter of fact . . . yes."

"I'm beginning to feel as though we're part of Her Majesty's Secret Service."

"Do you want to hear this, or not?"

"Sorry. Shell-shock, remember?"

"Uh-huh. Anyway, Hagen assured me that, for reasons undisclosed, the guards at the prison will be distracted and far from their normal positions. We go in the back door, which is near Kelsey's cell, and—"

"Kelsey?" Rafferty's ironic humor dissipated. Almost to himself, he muttered, "There can't be two of them in Hagen's organization, unless—Someone told me that Hagen's team was small, but I remember you said something once about it being large. Which is it?"

Sarah looked puzzled. "Well, the organization is large, but the team of field agents is fairly small. Why?"

"Then there can't be two Kelseys. Dammit, I know him."

"Is that good or bad?"

"Well, at least I know he's a good agent we can count on. And it makes this whole thing a bit more personal."

"He's the toy manufacturer from Billings. Sereno locked him up about three weeks ago, just one jump ahead of several enraged terrorists who were after his hide. The official American version is that he was arrested six weeks ago, when he reached Kadeira, but that isn't true. The press wasn't supposed to get hold of any of it, so a hasty statement was released when they did. Sereno unwittingly helped by arresting Kelsey before the terrorists could get their hands on him, and his version is that Kelsey committed 'crimes against the state.' A nice vague charge covering a multitude of possible sins."

Rafferty was frowning a little. "So if Kelsey hadn't been arrested, chances are good that the terrorist group would have killed him."

"Right. We must have somebody else undercover down here, because Kelsey hadn't gotten a chance to report before they grabbed him, but Hagen knew all this, and is very sure of his information. And then there are the keys; somebody got them for us, but who, nobody knows.

"Hagen says that Sereno is holding Kelsey despite the terrorists' demands that he be released to them. Sereno's argument—and the terrorist group has made it a public one around here—is that crimes against the state take precedence over everything else. He's in a pretty tough position. Apparently he isn't willing to hand over Kelsey, nor is he anxious to alienate the terrorists."

"Between a rock and a hard place," Rafferty murmured. He frowned at her, puzzled. "Sereno is claiming that Kelsey spied against his government as well as against the terrorist organization?"

"According to Hagen."

"Well, did he?"

"Spy on Sereno? Do you really think Hagen would have told me, true or not?"

Rafferty sighed. "Sorry. I wasn't using my head."

Sarah grinned a little. "Obviously."

He eyed her, then said, "You know, the deeper we get into this thing, the wilder it gets. Your boss is a frighteningly dangerous little man. I wonder why he's been allowed to live this long."

"Nobody could catch him?"

"You're probably right. By now, he ought to

have developed a strong sense of self-preservation." He sighed again. "So. After we bust Kelsey out—assuming we can—what happens then? I don't suppose a crack anti-terrorist squad will come swooping out of the clear blue and nobly hold off the bad guys while we make our getaway?"

"I told you we aren't supposed to be overt down here," Sarah said matter-of-factly and in a slightly reproving tone. She kept a straight face too.

Rafferty gave her a fascinated look. "Yes. Yes, you did tell me that, didn't you? I wonder why I'd forgotten. Um, what happens next?"

"We get him aboard the *Thespian* and sail out of here."

"Past all the nice armed boats?"

"Hagen says they won't be there."

Rafferty came over to sit beside her on the bed. He looked reflective, and his voice was gentle when he spoke. "Hagen says. Sarah love, I hope you're not putting too much faith in what Hagen says."

"Not much, no." She sighed. "He hasn't done too much to give me that kind of faith. At the same time, Rafferty, a part of me *does* believe him."

"The hell of it is, a part of me believes him too."

"He has a gun."

Sereno looked at Colonel Durant, amused. "Of course he has a gun. He's a wealthy man, and no fool. Stop worrying; Lewis will not try to harm me."

Durant, moving restlessly about the room, was

unconvinced. "It's a dangerous game you're playing, Andrés. If it blows up in your face, all will be lost."

Sereno leaned back in his chair and gazed across the neat desk at his aide and friend. "Perhaps. The timing is critical. And the secret to success, my friend, is illusion. Outside this house, my enemies think themselves friends, and my friends believe they are enemies."

"You can't satisfy both," Durant protested, and his tone held the sound of an old argument.

"I can, and will. For a time, I need my enemies. In the future, I will need my friends. I may go to bed with the devil, Vicente, but he would not be the first lover betrayed in the light of day."

Durant turned, and a smile lightened his thin face. "True. It is, as always, your game. I'll leave you." He headed for the door, then hesitated. "About the other . . . there is no word."

Sereno's face grew bleak. "No. I expected none."

"She looks very like—"

"Yes."

The colonel left quietly.

The president remained where he was for a long moment, staring into space. Then he swore softly and rose to his feet, his expression that of a man putting unbearable things out of his mind, at least for the time being.

But she *did* look like her. And he could use that, if he had to. No one who knew about her would doubt his motives—and nearly everyone on Kadeira knew about her. So that would serve as his excuse, should one be needed.

He crossed the room to a tall bookcase. Grasping one shelf, he pulled the entire structure away from the wall. Behind it was a hidden cavity, filled to capacity with electronic equipment.

He set several dials and switches and then placed a radio call, confident that it would be impossible for anyone other than his contact to hear the conversation, even if the correct frequency was stumbled upon.

Before his contact came on the line he thought of Adrian, the terrorist leader whose camp lay only a few miles inland. It was an odd alias for one who claimed Middle Eastern ties, but Sereno had heard stranger things. He had not, however, met a stranger man. Or a more dangerous one. Adrian was a pit viper with lethal venom, and Sereno didn't know how much longer he could hold the man at bay, away from his American prisoner.

The American prisoner was either a blessing or a curse, depending on how long Sereno could maneuver the dangerous pawns on his chessboard, and how quickly he could bring the game to a satisfactory conclusion.

"Go," a voice whispered from his receiver.

Depressing the call button, Sereno relayed his terse message.

Eight

That day and the next, Rafferty and Sarah remained at Sereno's home. They made no attempt to explore the city spread out below. Their host kept them company at times, and at others excused himself to disappear into his office with one or more of his men to do the work of running a country.

The two visitors had agreed privately that certain questions couldn't be asked of their host, but they also discovered that the island president willingly volunteered occasional information about his goals and even his methods. He made no apologies and no attempts to justify his actions; he merely explained the rationale behind them and left his listeners to make up their own minds.

And that became increasingly difficult.

"Now I know why Josh had trouble turning the man down," Rafferty said late the second night, as they lay close together in their bed. "He doesn't pull his punches or make any excuses at all for his behavior, and yet he's damned persuasive without trying to be. I almost could call those news stories about him and his government sheer propaganda."

Sarah moved closer to his side, frowning into the darkness. "I talked to his housekeeper while you were playing chess with him tonight. Her English was good, thank heaven, and she was the housekeeper to the former president as well as Sereno. She's not at all the type to worship blindly, but she adores him. And she says that things are much better now, in comparison to the state of the country under the last regime, I mean.

"She got very indignant when I told her the tales we've heard about the torture of political prisoners and the conscription of children for the military. For the first, she claims that political dissidents and revolutionaries are exiled, not imprisoned or tortured; she says the only political prisoner being held now is the American. For the second, she says Sereno would never conscript citizens, especially children, because he was taken into the revolutionary army himself as a teenager, totally against his will."

"Does she defend the lack of freedoms here?" Rafferty asked a bit dryly.

"In a way, yes. She says the newspaper and radio station were infiltrated by the rebels, and that both were inciting the citizens to murder. Not just overthrow Sereno, but actually to murder innocents. The president stopped that. He declared martial law because stores were being looted and public utilities sabotaged by the rebels."

Rafferty wasn't disbelieving of what she was telling him, just curious. "Then why'd we get hit with the vegetable salad on the drive up here?"

"Well, the one thing Sereno and his government simply can't do is get the economy back on its feet. Since the island hasn't been politically stable for more than fifty years, no foreign business will invest here, and the country has no industry. The farmers can't work because the rebels wreck their fields. The fishermen are able to feed the people, but that's it. And Sereno can't stabilize the mess long enough to get anything accomplished. Once in a blue moon he manages to get goods in for the shops, but the amount of money changing hands is pathetic."

"According to Maria, Sereno's feeding his people with the last few coins in the treasury. Or was, before the terrorists came here."

"Don't tell me they're helping the economy?"

"Indirectly, I suppose. They're paying money to Sereno to use the island as a base. If we believe Maria, he's using that money to try and get the country on its feet. And don't ask me how she knows all this."

"Servants always know."

"So I've heard."

Rafferty sighed. "If all this is true, and we'll assume it is, it explains why Sereno doesn't want to alienate the terrorists. But why hasn't he turned Kelsey over to them? He can't be protecting him."

"Why not? Kelsey's cover is solid as far as the

American press is concerned, and they'll raise hell if an innocent American citizen is handed over to terrorists. Sereno can't want that; if the American government comes down on him, and they'd have to unless they admit Kelsey *was* spying, he'd have a large, very powerful and angry country as an active enemy."

Rafferty chuckled suddenly. "It's a pity we can't tell him we're about to solve his problem for him. Assuming we can, of course."

"It has worked out well for him, hasn't it? If we get Kelsey out and off the island, Sereno can't be blamed for it. Except, of course, the terrorists can accuse him of negligence, or being too gullible in welcoming his houseguests. Sereno loses a dangerous prisoner, the terrorists lose a victim, and America gets back its 'innocent' citizen *and* information on the terrorist group—"

"And we get back to a normal life. Which I will definitely enjoy. Lord, this whole thing is insane. I feel like I'm in the middle of a nightmare."

"Well, thank you very much."

"You're the beautiful princess in the nightmare. It's the dragons and dungeons and wizards and enigmatic island presidents that are driving me nuts."

"I don't drive you nuts?" she asked innocently. "Why, just last night, you were saying—"

"Tonight too. Sarah!"

"That is the most *amazing* physiological response. And to such a simple action too. I really think—"

What she thought was lost in the growl of a physiological response of no mean order.

The next few days were more of a strain on them than they realized at first. They were new lovers, totally committed to one another and involved in that ongoing process, and they were a team entirely responsible for the success or failure of a delicate and dangerous mission. They could not be one or the other, they had to be both.

It was a fragile high-wire balancing act, demanding enormous equilibrium and a frightening amount of nerve. At times they could put the assignment out of their minds for a little while and think only of each other, but never for long. And they were, by necessity, guarded in what they said except when they were alone together.

Rafferty held up fairly well under the strain, automatically harnessing his analytical mind to observe and ponder. Stress had never bothered him much; he dealt with it well. And patience was an inherent trait strengthened by his chosen profession, so their enforced wait for action was no more than a mild irritant.

For Sarah, it was more difficult. Her life had not prepared her for this. She had not been trained for it. The first detachment had worn off quickly, leaving behind it uncertainty and anxiety. And compounding that was her ambivalence about Sereno. With every hour spent in his company, she found him more complex. And it touched her soft heart to realize that he was just the slightest bit ill at ease in her presence, as though looking at her was a constant reminder of something painful.

But even more, now that she and Rafferty were here and awaiting the signal to move, she found old doubts creeping back. The fear that she would not measure up, that she would somehow make a mistake and get both of them killed, haunted her.

And she worried about Kelsey, particularly since she'd found out that Rafferty knew him; before, he hadn't quite been real to her. She worried that he might be hurt, possibly tortured or deprived of food or water, even though Hagen had assured her that that would not be the case. It wasn't entirely wise to believe everything Hagen said, after all.

There was strength in Rafferty's love, and she held on to it fiercely, but she refused to burden him with her own uncertainties. It was important to her that she come to terms with this herself, that she work her way through it.

But it wasn't easy.

Zach and Lucas, in the cramped interior of the fishing boat's cockpit, watched as storm clouds seemed to roll across the water toward them.

Glancing down at the instruments, Zach said, "Barometer's near bottom. It's going to be a hell of a storm."

"Can we ride it out?"

"Sure." Zach glanced at his friend. "If I were the

commander of Sereno's fleet, I'd take my ships farther out to sea. There are reefs all around the island. It'd be dangerous to stay in close during a storm."

Lucas was silent for a moment, and then he smiled. "Sound strategy, I'd say. Lovely, isn't it?"

"Convenient, anyway." He pulled out a map of the island, spreading it across the instruments and frowning down at it. Pointing with one finger, he said, "Here looks good. It's not so close to the bay, but there's an inlet. And it's close to both Sereno's house and the prison."

Lucas nodded agreement, then looked at Zach curiously. "What made you think there was more to this than an exchange of information?"

"Not sure. The feeling that Sarah was holding something back, I suppose. And just a general sense of caution when it comes to Hagen's elaborate plans. It was enough to want to ask some pointed questions. I figure Josh could reach Hagen easier than we could." He chuckled suddenly. "Did you get the feeling when Josh called us back that he'd surprised our federal friend?"

"I got that feeling. D'you suppose it was the first time anyone managed to find Hagen when he didn't want to be found? I'll bet he has a healthy respect now for Josh's intelligence connections. Anyway, he must have been rattled, since he spilled the beans so quickly."

Zach glanced back up at the approaching storm. "Well, at least now we know. Think those rebels in the hills would use a storm for cover in attacking the town?"

"I think," Lucas said solemnly, "it'd be a crying shame to waste a good storm. All it would take to galvanize Sereno's soldiers would be some gunfire uncomfortably close to the town, and maybe blowing up an already abandoned building or two. How's your guerrilla mentality?"

Zach was smiling, but it was a smile that would have made anyone but a close friend nervous. "Flourishing, I believe." he cocked an eyebrow at Lucas. "Let's tell Hagen what we're going to do. I want to hear him sputter."

A considerable distance away and several hundred feet beneath the surface of the Caribbean, a rotund little man with the face of a cherub and a regrettable taste in suits sat back in his chair and smiled complacently. Not his original plan. No, he thought, but the amendments were working out very well.

There was a knock at the door of the radio room of the submarine, deserted but for Hagen, and the commander poked his head in. "New orders, sir?"

Still lost in his self-congratulation, Hagen replied, "No, maintain our position, Captain. Only a few more hours now, I think."

Left alone again, he gazed off into space and shook his head, feeling a little sad. It would be a shame, he thought, to lose the appreciable talents of Josh Long and his men. They really were quite resourceful. But he could hardly hope to draft each one more than once as a primary agent, since they seemed less prone now to trust him. Still, they had an endearing habit of spontaneously teaming up to help one another, which came in handy since Hagen's forces were spread somewhat thin to be effective in certain situations. And he kept *losing* agents, dammit, particularly female ones. He'd have to come up with another plan to be sure and avoid that next time.

But for the moment, he was definitely pleased. Provided Sereno reacted as planned, Zach Steele's silkily-reported intentions should do the trick nicely. Hagen smiled as he recalled that deep, polite voice that had all but dared him to object. He had, of course, objected on cue, and had certainly been convincing about it. But Steele and Kendrick really should have understood him better.

He'd known they would be involved. And the storm, well, that was hardly a surprise. The approach of a storm could be plotted days in advance, and it was patently obvious that such an event should be used to advantage. And how better to use nature's sound and fury than as a cover for sly rebel forces—even if *they* didn't think of it.

No appreciation for genius, he thought, that was it.

Hagen looked around at the cramped room, half expecting plaudits for his brilliance. The fact that he was alone bothered him not at all.

He heard the applause.

The storm had reached full strength by morning, and Sarah watched through the French doors of the book-lined den as wind and rain lashed the trees and plants out in the garden. She was alone in the room since Rafferty had gone to the kitchen to assuage a sudden stab of midmorning hunger. He'd probably charm Maria, who was already beginning to beam when she saw him.

Sarah smiled. He was a charming man, her Rafferty.

She turned as the door opened, and tensed a little when she saw Andrés Sereno.

"Am I intruding?" he asked with a smile. "You looked very thoughtful."

"Just enjoying the storm," she told him, managing to keep her voice easy.

"Yes, the storms here are spectacular. This isn't a particularly dangerous one, however." Not a man to sit while a woman stood, he leaned against one of the bookshelves and slid his hands into his pockets, watching her. "I met Rafferty on his way to the kitchen."

"I think he just wanted to flirt with Maria," she said, thinking how easily the president had gotten on a first-name basis with them. Just part of the man's appeal.

"Perhaps. He is obviously much in love with his wife." Seeing her expression cool, he added quietly, "You must forgive the personal observation; my people treasure love."

Sarah gazed out the window without offering a response.

"You don't approve of me, do you, Sarah?" There was a slight hesitation before he spoke her name.

"It isn't my place to approve or disapprove."

"But you nonetheless consider me a ruthless dictator."

She gestured helplessly, unwilling to be drawn into this conversation, yet unable to stop it. "I've heard that you allow terrorists to live here." It was the worst she knew of him, and what bothered her more than all the rest.

"That news has spread." His tone was remote. "Would you believe me and understand, I wonder, if I told you that I hate terrorism?"

She turned to look at him. "No, I wouldn't."

His black eyes were unreadable. "Of course not. Neither would they."

Sarah frowned a little, aware that there was some undercurrent in his voice, some subtlety she was missing. There was a pattern, and her puzzle-oriented mind quite abruptly began putting pieces in place. Some pieces seemed wrong, had always seemed wrong, yet they fit neatly, if she accepted one absolutely wild supposition as fact. But it couldn't be—could it?

Sarah looked into those waiting black eyes, and she almost felt reckless enough to ask him the question. Almost. But she didn't ask, because as long as he didn't deny what she now believed, much of her confusion regarding him was gone, and she preferred it that way.

Shades of gray.

She focused on what he was saying.

"I've found it's useless to regret. Had your friend Joshua Long chosen to invest here, perhaps the situation would be different. Or perhaps not. I certainly don't blame him. People don't change, after all, and rebellion was in the air even then. My country has been cursed with weak, ineffectual leaders for too much of its history. I don't intend to become a part of that curse. I will be a dictator, Sarah Lewis, and ruthless until my country is whole again."

Sarah realized she was smiling, but whatever she might have said in response to his declaration was lost as Rafferty came into the room. He was frowning, and spoke quickly to Sereno.

"There were some shots a few minutes ago. We could hear them on the other side of the house. Sounded like they came from the middle of the city."

Before the president could respond, they all heard the explosion in the distance and felt a slight tremor. A second explosion followed quickly.

Sereno's face was expressionless. "The rebels must be using the storm as cover. That definitely came from the city."

Colonel Durant, who was almost constantly in the house, entered the room not five minutes later. His face was grim as he reported what had happened. "A warehouse and the old hotel were hit. Both bombed before, both deserted. Harassment."

Sereno returned his colonel's gaze. Softly, he said. "They wanted to catch us off guard. Colonel, order all men to form a cordon around the city. Use the harbor patrol and prison guards as well as those patrolling the city. We'll tighten the net as we move toward the center of the city, and perhaps capture a few rebels."

Durant saluted quickly and left.

Sereno looked at his houseguests with faint apology. "If you'll excuse me, this is something I'm afraid I must see to personally." His eyes focused on Sarah very intently. "You'll be safe," he finished abruptly, and strode from the room, closing the door behind him.

Rafferty moved to her side and looked at his watch. "Half past eleven," he murmured. "We could be at the prison by twelve. Think this is it?"

"The prison guards are being pulled away from their posts," she said. "And the harbor guards. There'll never be a better time. I think—"

One of the French doors swung open suddenly, admitting a gust of wind, what seemed like a gallon of rain, and two drenched Americans. With one eye on the hall doors, Zach said softly, "Hope you've got a key to the cell."

"We're out of explosives," Lucas explained cheerfully.

Sarah looked at Rafferty. "D'you think this is the 'unmistakable signal' we're waiting for?"

"It works for me," Rafferty replied blankly, staring at his friends.

They had been prepared to leave their possessions behind, and since Lucas had a gun for Rafferty he didn't bother going back upstairs. His friends waited in the stormy garden, and Rafferty and Sarah waited tensely in the den, until they heard Sereno and his colonel leave the house.

Several moments later they headed for the prison.

• • •

It was hardly an easy trip. They were battered by the storm, and at one point had to seek shelter behind a stone wall while soldiers passed within ten feet of them. But they managed to reach the prison without incident.

They found, after carefully studying the building, that the guards, if any, were all on the inside, since none were visible outside. The back door was just where it was supposed to be, and Sarah's key fit perfectly. The door opened into a short hallway with thick doors at either end. One door led to the main part of the building, and Zach stood guard there. Lucas remained at the outer door—they both had their weapons at the ready—and Sarah and Rafferty went in search of Kelsey's cell.

The door they passed through led them along a corridor, down a flight of stone steps, and past several unoccupied cells that were depressing in their tiny size and utter bleakness. So both Sarah and Rafferty were braced for the worst when her second key unlocked the door of Kelsey's cell.

He was there. He was lying back on a comfortable bunk and reading a magazine from the light of a lamp with a fringed shade. There were several magazines on the floor beside the bunk. He was drinking from a bottle of beer.

He looked up when the door opened, his brows rising faintly, an expression of amiable surprise on his lean face. "Hello. Taking shelter from the storm?"

Rafferty didn't know whether to be relieved because his worst fears had been definitely off-base, or annoyed to find the subject of all their efforts entirely undamaged and lazily comfortable in his so-called cell. "Can't you recognize the cavalry when you see it?" he demanded.

Kelsey sat up on his bunk and swung his long legs to the floor, reaching for his shoes, grinning now. "Took you long enough, I must say."

"Go to hell," Rafferty told him politely.

"I hate to interrupt this mutual admiration society—" Sarah began.

"Hey, Rafferty, you're keeping better company these days," Kelsey observed after looking Sarah over thoroughly. He got to his feet and ostentatiously tucked in his shirt.

"Zach and Lucas are here, too."

Kelsey sighed. "You know, Hagen truly amazes me. He's actually as great as he thinks he is. And if you tell him I said that, I'll deny it."

"He does seem to get all his puppets onstage for his little plays, doesn't he?"

"He does at that. It's depressing, isn't it? And it's rather frightening when you think about it. It's to my credit that I don't, often."

"If you're ready?"

"Delighted."

"After you, then."

"As it should be."

Sarah had been listening and watching them as though they were out of their minds, but a part of her recognized the sheer release of tension. So she wasn't totally surprised to see Kelsey leave his cell with suave dignity, or to see Rafferty follow behind gravely.

Men were strange creatures.

Humor fell by the wayside as they hurried cautiously toward the harbor. They could hear automatic gunfire uncomfortably close, and Rafferty struggled to ask Zach a question that wouldn't be snatched away by the wind.

"If you guys started the phony attack, who the hell are they shooting at?" He held Sarah's hand tightly as they all pushed against the wind and rain.

"You've got me," Zach answered. "Maybe shadows. Or each other. Just hope they keep shooting and stay occupied. We don't want them getting restless."

"Where, by the way, did you get the explosives?"

"Forethought. Brought 'em with us."

Sarah, suddenly worried, said, "What if the *Thespian* isn't tied up at the dock? With the storm—"

"It's there," Lucas told her. "We saw it when we set the charges in town. Tied up short and riding rough, but definitely there. The crew must be seasick by now." He looked at Zach and asked, "What about our fishing boat?"

Zach grunted. "We'll leave it. And send Hagen a bill for it later."

Lucas nodded approvingly. "Nice touch."

"Is Sereno with his men?" Kelsey asked, when they paused to peer around the corner of a building.

"Yes, he left the house with Colonel Durant," Rafferty told him. "Why?"

"Oh, no reason."

Rafferty gave him a sharp look, but didn't probe.

"The harbor looks clear," Zach reported, his eyes scanning the area carefully from where they stood near the corner of a warehouse. "Nothing's moving at all."

Cheerfully, Kelsey said, "I'm ready to shake the dust of this place off my feet. Let's go."

They went.

When an overeager lieutenant reported he'd seen several men and a woman heading for the harbor, Sereno resisted the urge to deck the young officer. Given a choice, he would have simply ignored the information, but too many ears had heard for that to be a viable option.

He avoided Durant's worried eyes, merely commanding a small group of soldiers to come with him to the harbor. He chose them by name, quickly but very carefully, selecting only those he was certain would obey him instantly no matter what the command. They also just happened to be men who had known the other Sara.

Then he led the way.

Sereno set a deliberate pace, not too fast, keeping close to buildings. He held his sidearm in one hand, but cautioned his men to hold their fire until ordered otherwise.

There was nothing more he could do.

The American party reached the dock, where the

Thespian was indeed tied up and riding the storm-tossed waters. As they ran toward the yacht, the engine thrummed to life. Tom and Dick appeared from the bridge as though summoned, and readied to cast off.

It was then that Zach, preparing to leap aboard the rising and falling deck of the yacht, glanced back the way they had come and froze.

Almost as if nature herself controlled the storm for the benefit of drama, the rain stopped abruptly and the wind ceased to howl. So that when they all looked at what had caught Zach's attention, they could see all too clearly.

President Andrés Sereno stood not twenty feet away heading a small group of soldiers. And the businesslike automatic he held, was pointed at them. At, specifically, the person nearest to him—Sarah.

They were all frozen for a moment, until one of Sereno's men began to lift his gun. Without looking at him, the president snapped a harsh command in Spanish, and the soldier lowered his gun instantly.

Rafferty moved then, quickly pulling Sarah behind him and speaking to Zach in a low voice. "Get her on the yacht." He didn't take his eyes off Sereno. The president didn't move, but he didn't lower his gun, either.

He could hear the sounds of the others boarding the yacht, but continued to look at Sereno. After what seemed an eternity, that unwavering gun finally lowered, and a second command was barked out to the men. Silently, they backed up another twenty feet, then stood ready. And there was no rebellion on those faces, only understanding. Sereno stood still for a moment longer, then decisively holstered his pistol, turned on his heel, and strode away. His men fell in behind him as he passed, and within seconds they were gone.

Rafferty released breath he hadn't realized he was holding, then quickly boarded the yacht. "Let's get out of here before he changes his mind," he told the others.

As the *Thespian* pulled away from the dock and headed out to sea, Rafferty held Sarah tightly and listened to the words that were nearly lost against his chest.

"Macho. Stupidly macho, but I knew he wouldn't shoot you."

"Oddly enough," Rafferty said, "I knew he wouldn't too."

Nine

"You're all damned lucky you didn't get killed." Josh Long's voice was very definite.

The group assembled in the luxurious main "cabin" of the *Corsair* tried in various ways to look properly contrite, but none of them pulled it off. Except for the captain and crew of the *Thespian*, who were all on their way back to Trinidad, everyone involved in the matter was present.

Everyone, that was, except for Hagen, who had a lively sense of self-preservation, and the long-suffering Kelsey, who had elected to return with the crew of the *Thespian*.

Sarah, safe in the circle of Rafferty's arm, studied them all with thoughtfully appraising eyes, particularly the two she'd just met.

Joshua Long had surprised her a little. For a captain of industry he was absurdly young, somewhere in his mid-thirties, she thought, and remarkably casual and informal for all his wealth and power. He was also every woman's dream. He was tall, dark, and handsome, although his face, she thought, could be hard if he chose.

He didn't choose to appear hard when he looked at his friends with a faintly exasperated expression of camaraderie, nor when he looked at his wife—which was often.

Raven Long was a tall, striking brunette with violet eyes and a warm voice. She was naturally graceful, instinctively charming, and completely spontaneous. Within ten minutes of their coming aboard, she had sworn at all three of her husband's friends for disturbing their honeymoon, instantly followed with a demand to be told what had happened on Kadeira, and finished up by cheerfully damning Hagen and asking Rafferty when the wedding would occur.

Interrupted honeymoon or no, both Josh and Raven were obviously in no need of cementing the first critical stage of a marriage. Their shared glances held the warm glow of a deep and abiding love, and their plain gold wedding bands were worn with the ineffable look of permanence and certainty.

Basking in the glow of her own love, Sarah listened as Rafferty responded to Josh's statement.

"Well, you could have helped us out a little more, you know. That cryptic remark about 'shades of gray' wasn't very much to go on."

"I was almost completely going on instinct," Josh told him. "And I met him several years ago, after all. An afternoon's conversation. He was ruthless then, and I knew damned well *that* hadn't changed. Still, there was just something about the man." He looked at Sarah and smiled. "He turned his back and let you walk away."

She nodded. "I had a feeling he might. And I think I'll call his Sara when we get back. She might like to know that."

"I think you're right," Josh told her, smiling at this delicate lady who had captured Rafferty's heart.

Rafferty looked steadily at his friend and boss. "Hagen had no right to ask you to do what you did. And, dammit, you had no business at all agreeing to it! Josh, when Sereno calls in that favor—"

Joshua Long lifted a cool eyebrow at him, at that moment every inch the tough businessman, and said calmly, "He won't ask for more than I'm willing to give."

"How can you be sure of that?"

"Fifteen years spent in boardrooms."

"Josh, he's a *dictator.*"

"He's a businessman."

Interrupting what promised to be a standoff between Josh and Rafferty, Raven said in a cheerful voice, "I think we should celebrate."

"Our survival?" Zach asked.

Raven made a rude noise. "You guys are like cats—you always land on your feet. No, we'll celebrate Sarah and Rafferty's forthcoming marriage."

So they broke out the champagne.

A considerable time later, in the cabin allotted to them, Sarah blissfully allowed Rafferty to undress her. She couldn't help, mainly because she had celebrated with a future bride's happy enthusiasm and was, therefore, wonderfully limp and unconcerned.

Another word for it would have been "drunk."

"You have no head for champagne," Rafferty observed, sliding Raven's borrowed jeans down Sarah's lovely legs with difficulty, while those legs moved to some imaginary music.

She sat up abruptly on the bed and made a grab for him, looking puzzled when she missed. "Where did you go?"

"Right here, darling," he muttered, unbuttoning her blouse and trying not to laugh. This side of his Sarah was definitely endearing and somewhat fascinating. He didn't think he'd ever forget the image of her standing before Zach, so tiny next to his bulk, while she solemnly reproved him for having deceived Rafferty years before.

It was mean, she'd said.

Zach had looked rather sheepish, which was astonishing in itself.

Sarah peered at him owlishly. "You weren't there a minute ago, dammit."

"Sorry about that."

She blinked, then squinted. "Which one *are* you?" she asked, apparently afflicted with a distressing case of double—or triple—vision.

"The one in the middle," he told her gently.

She let him remove her blouse, then aimed carefully with both hands and managed to find his face. "There you are. Hello."

"Hi." Stoically, he removed her bra and then pulled a borrowed nightgown over her head.

"You're dressing me," she realized.

"Uh-huh."

"But that isn't right. Don't you want to ravish a drunken wanton?" she asked, then repeated the question to herself as if it didn't make sense.

"I want you to take a little nap."

"But I'm not sleepy."

"Lie back and close your eyes, and I promise you'll be sleepy. Trust me."

"But it isn't even dark yet."

"This too shall pass. Go to sleep, darling."

Drifting away, Sarah said sleepily, "It doesn't work when you say it, does it? Only when I say it."

"Only when you say it, darling," he agreed tenderly.

"Trinidad looks different," she said, "when you aren't here pretending to be something you're not."

Rafferty joined her on the balcony, slipping his arms around her and pulling her back against him. "I've noticed," he agreed. "So, Mrs. Lewis, you're enjoying your honeymoon?"

"If you have to ask, Harvard produced a dud."

"A little reassurance never hurts," he murmured, nuzzling her neck.

"Then be reassured. I've never been happier." She smiled and covered the hands lying on her stomach with her own. "And your idea of honeymooning here was just perfect. We couldn't have found a better place."

He hugged her. A little curious, he said, "I never

asked, but what did Hagen say when you asked for the time off?"

"That I'd earned it. He seemed relieved when I told him I wasn't quitting, just transferring to the New York office. He said, by the way, and very reprovingly, that he really didn't think he—meaning the agency—should have to pay for a fishing boat."

"To which you replied?"

"I told him to take it up with Zach."

"I don't imagine he will."

"Hardly. He signed a voucher on the spot."

"Ummm. I don't suppose you asked him—?"

Sarah turned to gaze up at him, smiling. "No. I guess I was afraid he'd deny it."

Rafferty touched her cheek lightly. "You really did care about Sereno, didn't you? You don't want him to be a dyed-in-the-wool villain."

Not for the first time during the last few weeks, Sarah tried to get it clear in her own mind. "It's just that what I believe makes so much *sense*. I'm not saying he would have let us escape if it hadn't benefited him in some way, but I have to believe he was glad that's how it worked out.

"Just think about it. He arrested Kelsey just before the terrorists would have gotten him and killed him, even though Kelsey hadn't done anything at all to justify the charge of spying on Sereno's government. Kelsey was treated more like a guest than a prisoner. Sereno refused to turn him over to the terrorists, even though he supposedly wanted and needed their goodwill.

"And then there are the keys. Who but Sereno

could have not only gotten them, but also *got them to Hagen.* I don't think we had a second agent in Kadeira. I think Sereno himself was in touch with Hagen, and more or less told him to get his agent the hell out of the country before Kelsey got himself killed and Sereno was blamed for it."

"It makes sense," Rafferty admitted. "Especially if he wanted to get Kelsey's information out of the country as well as his dangerous hide."

"I really believe that he hates terrorists. Remember what I told you about that last day, and what he said to me? That's when it all started to make sense to me. Shades of gray. He'd allow terrorists to have a base in his country and take money from them for the privilege, pour the money into his economy, and then help get information about the organization out to people who intend to stop them.

"And all the while, he had perfectly logical explanations to hand the terrorists. Kelsey was in jail on a legitimate charge. We were there because Sereno was eager to do a very powerful man a simple favor. A very believable attack by the rebels drew his soldiers away from the prison which allowed us to break Kelsey out. And at the end . . ."

"At the end," Rafferty finished, "he simply couldn't allow the image of the woman he loved to come to any harm. Something his men very obviously knew, judging by their faces. So he turned his back and walked away."

Sarah nodded. "So he comes out on top. The terrorists are angry but unsuspicious. Joshua Long owes him a favor. *Hagen* owes him a favor. And, best of all, America isn't up in arms against him."

Thinking of the terrorists, Rafferty said, "He's still in bed with the devil, though."

Smiling, she said, "I'm not trying to paint him *all* white, you know. I just don't think he's a monster anymore."

"You were smiling at him that last day," Rafferty remembered. "As if you finally understood him, and weren't worried about it anymore."

"That's about the way it was."

"I wanted to deck him."

Surprised, she said, "It didn't show."

"I'm a great poker player."

"Darling, you know—"

"Oh, lord," he muttered, bending his head to capture her lips. And when he carried her into their bedroom, it was caveman style, over one shoulder.

"You said that deliberately," Rafferty decided sometime later in a drained voice.

Sarah raised herself on an elbow to smile down at him, mischief sparkling in her sea-green eyes. "Don't be ridiculous."

"You did. I was well on my way to developing an inferiority complex regarding Sereno, and you set out to cure me of it. And very nicely, too."

"Well," she said innocently, "when a woman knows which button to push, it's a little hard to resist pushing."

He opened one eye and stared at her. "Yeah."

She giggled. "You remember when we were celebrating on the *Corsair*? I almost said it then."

"I know you did. That's why I kissed you and then managed to get you to our cabin so fast." He sighed. "I can just see what's going to happen. Every time we have a fight, you'll look at me with those lovely eyes and call me darling, and I'll forget my name."

"I could call you at the office—"

"Don't you dare! At least, don't call me darling over the phone. I'd kill myself getting home to you."

"Or show up in court—"

"I won't tell you when I'm going to be in court. Besides, I don't have to be there often these days."

"Boardrooms instead?"

He looked at her warily.

Sarah giggled. "I won't, I promise. Besides, if you push a button too often, it'll wear out. I wouldn't want that, now would I?"

Rafferty pulled her over on top of him, smiling. "I hope not." His eyes narrowed slightly. "And I wonder if you have a button."

"Of course not," she denied stoutly.

"No?"

Absolutely not."

After a few moments, she added breathlessly, "Well, not a verbal one, at any rate."

Rafferty smiled.

Epilogue

"You've lost another agent," Kelsey said cheerfully. "A field agent, that is. You won't be able to get Sarah out of an office again. And since Rafferty has your number now, boss, you sure as hell won't be able to con him again."

"Most unfortunate." Hagen frowned at the clear blue water of the Caribbean, his mind, as always, refusing to allow him to relax and enjoy the vacation. "I would have said such an eventuality was highly improbable given the information—"

"The lies," Kelsey translated dryly, "you told them."

He was splendidly ignored.

"It appears I underestimated Rafferty Lewis's intuitive abilities," Hagen decided. "He discovered far sooner than anticipated that I had—misled him about Miss Cavell's past."

"Tragic past," Kelsey reminded politely, thoroughly enjoying his boss's unusual lapse from godlike omniscience.

Again, he was ignored.

"The human element." Hagen muttered the phrase several times, clearly searching for a way around this annoying stumbling block in the path of his greatness.

Kelsey leaned his head back, taking advantage of the warm sunlight. "Let me know," he advised, "when you find a way around that one."

Long moments passed, and then Hagen said dreamily, "My boy, there is nothing that cannot be surmounted with enough forethought and planning."

Kelsey turned his head and opened one eye to peer at his boss. "Uh-huh. Who's next?"

"Zachary Steele."

THE EDITOR'S CORNER

I AM DELIGHTED TO WELCOME KATE HARTSON AS YOUR AUTHOR OF THIS MONTH'S EDITOR'S CORNER, AND TO LET YOU KNOW THAT NORA ROBERTS'S NEXT SIZZLING ROMANTIC SUSPENSE NOVEL—**SACRED SINS**—WILL COME OUT NEXT MONTH.

HAPPY HOLIDAYS!

Carolyn Nichols

I'm delighted to have joined the LOVESWEPT team as Senior Editor to work on these fabulous romances, and I'm glad to be writing the Editor's Corner this month so that I can say *hi* to all of you.

Isn't it a treat having six LOVESWEPT books every month? We never have to be without a LOVESWEPT in the bedroom, den, or purse. And now there are enough of these luscious stories to last through the month!

Soon we'll be rushing into the holiday season, full of sharing and good cheer. We have some special LOVESWEPT books to share—our holiday gifts to you!

RAINBOW RYDER, LOVESWEPT #222, by Linda Hampton, is a gift of excitement, as our respectable heroine, Kathryn Elizabeth Asbury, a pillar of the community, finds herself attracted to Ryder Malone, a wildly handsome rogue who has a penchant for riding motorcycles. Kathryn's orderly life is shaken by Ryder, who isn't quite what he appears to be. She fights hard for control

(continued)

but really can't resist this wild and free-spirited "King of the Road." Then she makes a thrilling discovery—and falling hard doesn't hurt a bit. **RAINBOW RYDER** is sure to be one of your favorites, but don't stop reading, we have five more LOVESWEPT GIFTS for you. . . .

Diamonds are the gift in Glenna McReynolds's **THIEVES IN THE NIGHT,** LOVESWEPT #223—how appropriate for the holiday season! Our heroine, Chantal Cochard, is an ex-jewel thief forced out of retirement when her family's prize diamond necklace shows up around some other woman's neck. DIAMONDS may be a girl's best friend, but they're not her lover. That's better left to well-built, sexy men like our hero, Jaz Peterson. Once Chantal invites him into her Aspen hideaway, she quickly learns that love is the most precious jewel of all!

Witty Linda Cajio's gift to us is **DOUBLE DEALING,** LOVESWEPT #224, a story of childhood dreams and adult surrender. Our heroine, Rae Varkely, mistress of a fabulous estate, is forced into a position where she simply has to kidnap Jed Waters. She makes a ransom demand, but our hero refuses to be released! Making demands of his own, he turns the tables on Rae, who can't help but pay with her heart. Still she has to protect her property from Jed's plans for development. But Jed has no intention of destroying anything—he only wants to build a strong relationship with the mistress of the manor.

A new book from Kay Hooper is always a gift, but **ZACH'S LAW,** LOVESWEPT #225, is an especially wonderful one. As the tale continues of those incredible men who work for Joshua Logan (and who indirectly fall out of SERENA'S WEB), we meet petite Teddy Tyler stranded on a deserted mountain road. Zach Steele, a strong, silent type who frightens Teddy because he ignites such strong desire in her, is her rescuer . . . then her sweet jailer . . . and the captive of her love. But Hagen's got his claws into Zach, there's mayhem on the horizon, and there's Zach's own past to confront before true love can win out!

(continued)

Sara Orwig's **OUT OF A MIST,** LOVESWEPT #226, is a gift of desire, as Millie and Ken are reunited after a brief but unforgettable encounter. Ken is on the run from the law, and Millie discovers him wounded and hiding in her closet. Of course, she knows he's done nothing wrong and she lets him stay with her until they can clear his name. But the longer he stays, the more he finds a place in her heart. Millie blossoms in Ken's embrace, but Ken won't settle for just passion—his desire is the lasting kind!

Our final romantic gift for you is a wonderful new book by Patt Buchiester called **TWO ROADS,** LOVESWEPT #227. This moving book is a story of healing: Nicole Piccolo is recovering from a broken leg and a broken heart, trying to forget Clay Masters, the man who promised her *forever* and then disappeared from her life. When Clay reappears a year later, the wounds are opened again, but Clay is determined to show Nicole that he never meant to leave and his heart has always been hers. When the healing is complete, they begin again with no pain to mar the exquisite pleasure of being in love.

Enjoy our gifts to you, sent with love and good cheer from your LOVESWEPT authors and editors!

Kate Hartson

Kate Hartson
Editor
LOVESWEPT
Bantam Books, Inc.
666 Fifth Avenue
New York, NY 10103